BARGAINING WITH THE LADY OF MEREWOOD

The Ladies of the Keep, Book Two

(Connected to The Lords of Vice Series
and The Duke's Guard Series)

C.H. Admirand

© Copyright 2023 by C.H. Admirand
Text by C.H. Admirand
Cover by Dar Albert

Dragonblade Publishing, Inc. is an imprint of Kathryn Le Veque Novels, Inc.
P.O. Box 23
Moreno Valley, CA 92556
ceo@dragonbladepublishing.com

Produced in the United States of America

Revised Editions October 2024, July 2018, October 2014
Previous Edition Published April 2007
Trade Paperback Edition

Reproduction of any kind except where it pertains to short quotes in relation to advertising or promotion is strictly prohibited.

All Rights Reserved.

The characters and events portrayed in this book are fictitious. Any similarity to real persons, living or dead, is purely coincidental and not intended by the author.

ARE YOU SIGNED UP FOR DRAGONBLADE'S BLOG?

You'll get the latest news and information on exclusive giveaways, exclusive excerpts, coming releases, sales, free books, cover reveals and more.

Check out our complete list of authors, too!

No spam, no junk. That's a promise!

Sign Up Here
www.dragonbladepublishing.com

Dearest Reader;

Thank you for your support of a small press. At Dragonblade Publishing, we strive to bring you the highest quality Historical Romance from some of the best authors in the business. Without your support, there is no 'us', so we sincerely hope you adore these stories and find some new favorite authors along the way.

Happy Reading!

CEO, Dragonblade Publishing

Additional Dragonblade books by Author C.H. Admirand

The Ladies of the Keep Series
Liberating the Lady of Loughmoe (Book 1)
Bargaining with the Lady of Merewood (Book 2)
Rescuing the Lady of Sedgeworth (Book 3)

The Duke's Guard Series
The Duke's Sword (Book 1)
The Duke's Protector (Book 2)
The Duke's Shield (Book 3)
The Duke's Dragoon (Book 4)
The Duke's Hammer (Book 5)
The Duke's Defender (Book 6)
The Duke's Saber (Book 7)
The Duke's Enforcer (Book 8)
The Duke's Mercenary (Book 9)

The Lords of Vice Series
Mending the Duke's Pride (Book 1)
Avoiding the Earl's Lust (Book 2)
Tempering the Viscount's Envy (Book 3)
Redirecting the Baron's Greed (Book 4)
His Vow to Keep (Novella)
The Merry Wife of Wyndmere (Novella)

The Lyon's Den Series
Rescued by the Lyon
Captivated by the Lyon
The Lyon's Saving Grace

Historical Cookbook
Dragonblade's Historical Recipe Cookbook:
Recipes from some of your favorite Historical Romance Authors

Dedication

This book is dedicated to Kathryn Le Veque, CEO of Dragonblade Publishing, Inc., author extraordinaire, and friend. You gave me a reason to carry on when my life fell apart and helped me keep my promise to my Heavenly Hubby to finish the Lords of Vice series and continue to promote my books.

I will be forever grateful for your compassion, understanding, and a place within the Dragonblade Family. You helped me to find a purpose in my life again, and a place where I can imbue my hardheaded Dragonblade heroes with some of DJ's best qualities: his honesty, his integrity, his compassion for others, and his killer broad shoulders—and introduce them to my feisty Dragonblade heroines. Thank you!

Ancient Viking Prophecy...

If a woman finds love after thirty summers, 'twill burn hotter than the fires that forged Thor's great hammer!

Love grows with age, deepens through life's triumphs and tragedies. If we embrace life, and meet it head on, love doesn't have to end when loved ones depart this life.

We hold them forever in our hearts, where they give us the strength to carry on...and love again.

Aut Vincam, Aut Periam... I will either conquer or perish!

Prologue

1072 Northumbria

He traced the arch of her brow with his fingertip, then kissed it. His finger swept along the curve of her cheek, tracing the line of her jaw, and ending in the hollow at the base of her throat.

Her eyes drifted closed, and she softly smiled.

"Eyreka."

She opened her eyes and their gazes locked. The embers of his passion, still glowing, softened his stormy-gray gaze. By Odin, she loved him! He traced an X over her heart; it beat strong beneath his touch.

"Now and forever, Eyreka." He dipped his head and kissed the spot with a tenderness that brought tears to her eyes.

She knew then he was leaving, but the thought of never seeing him again, never touching him, formed a knot of anguish in her stomach. It tangled tighter and started to burn.

Though she knew it was hopeless, she held on with a grip of iron.

"I cannot come to you again." The softly uttered words tore a gaping wound in her already aching heart. "'Tis time for you to let go."

She gathered up the remnants of her tattered courage, knowing it would be the last time she saw him. Her hand shook as she traced an X over the ugly scar—the barrier that stood between them—the impenetrable wall between Valhalla and Earth. She tasted the salt of her own tears as she placed her lips where a Norman arrow had pierced the heart in her husband's breast.

"Now and forever, Addison," she whispered.

Her vow broke the hold she had on him. But this time he did not just disappear, a shaft of bright white light speared the darkness, glowing around him like an aura, making his broad warrior's frame look even larger.

She reached a hand out to touch him one last time.

He shook his head. "Nay, love. 'Tis time to go on with your life. Change is coming to Merewood Keep," he warned. "Do not let it defeat you. Remember your heritage, my Viking princess and meet it head on."

"Aye," she rasped.

The light flared behind him and went out. She bolted up in bed, reaching for him; her sleeping gown clinging to the curves of her sweat-drenched body. Her mind struggled to surface and broke through her dreams, only to face the stark reality that Addison was truly dead and gone, and the king had granted their home to a Norman baron.

CHAPTER ONE

"THE KING AWAITS."

The attendant's words burned themselves into Lady Eyreka's mind. Her hands trembled. She clasped them tighter together and nodded. Her mind whirled. Needing to concentrate and remember all she planned to say, she thought of her eldest son, Garrick, and his wife, Jillian. Their love had suffused itself into the very stones of Merewood Keep's foundations and was at the very heart of her people's existence.

This was her only chance.

"I cannot fail," she whispered. Her family's home was about to be wrested from their grasp and would be as if all Garrick and Jillian had gone through to rebuild was for naught.

She took a deep cleansing breath and hurried to catch up to the young servant. For the second time in her life, she would bargain with the gods in exchange for those she loved. Would this Norman be as eager to accept her as part of the spoils of war as her first husband had?

Her stomach clenched. She was no longer the innocent young woman who had bravely ridden into their enemy's embrace. She had three grown sons, and the scars to prove it. In a few months she would reach her fortieth summer.

As she walked along the corridor, she thought of all the reasons the Norman might accept her. The years had been kind to her. She still had all of her teeth and only a few wrinkles about her eyes. Looking down she frowned at the streaks of silvery-gray running through her hair.

Mayhap the years had not been as kind as she thought.

What man would want her, when he could have a much younger maid for a wife? Her footsteps echoed about her. Was her plan doomed before she had a chance to offer it? She clamped down on her traitorous thoughts when the attendant paused in front of a closed door. Before she could tell the young man she'd changed her mind, he opened the door with a flourish and bade her enter.

Fear speared through her, but she focused on the sight before her.

King William sat on a massive oak chair set on a dais. He was larger than she had imagined. His mien was arrogant, his very posture reeking of power. But it was not so much his size as the fierce frown on his face that terrified her. This man had the power to grant her desire, or have the head lifted from her shoulders with the wave of his hand.

At his nod to enter, she inclined her head and prayed her legs would cooperate. Though they wobbled, she hid that fact by walking slowly forward. At the edge of the dais, she sank to her knees in homage.

While she waited for him to recognize her show of fealty, her mind raced, caught up in a whirlwind of emotion. This man alone was responsible for the deaths of thousands of good Saxon thanes. Had he given the command to shoot the arrow that had ended her husband's life?

Her stomach churned and a sour, bilious taste surged up her throat, thinking of the ugly wound the Norman arrow had left behind. Though strong threads closed the cauterized wound, the arrow had pierced his heart. She had held her dying husband in her arms, whispering words of prayer to her own Viking gods and Addison's Christian god for good measure.

Time stood still while she remembered the shared pain that

connected her to Addison. Their love had made them well and truly one. His thoughts were her thoughts, his pain was her pain. She remembered feeling the sensation of icy cold hands clutching her aching stomach. Tears clogged her throat with each ragged breath she drew, then he breathed his last.

"Lady Eyreka," the king acknowledged her presence at last, motioning for her to rise. "You may speak."

Her head shot up. Heart pounding, she forced herself to let go of the past. She rose to her feet, returning to the present. The words she'd so carefully rehearsed snagged in her throat, drowned out by the loud hammering of her heart echoing through the silence of the room.

Impatience oozed from every pore in the ruddy king's body. Temper simmered in the hard gaze he leveled at her. "Well?"

I will not fail. "I wish to discuss my home, Merewood Keep."

William's eyes flashed briefly, but he motioned for her to continue.

"My son, Garrick, has received your missive regarding his replacement as lord of our holding."

"Then why has he not come before me?" the king demanded, his massive fist crashing down upon the arm of the chair.

"I … that is he …" she stammered, placing a hand to her breast. She felt Jillian's amber pendant and clutched it tightly. She said a quick prayer of thanks to her son's wife for insisting she borrow it, and another to the ancient ones who had inscribed the runes upon it.

Almost immediately a surge of warmth suffused her hand and traveled up her arm. She was filled with renewed confidence that her plan was going to succeed. Her gaze darted back to her king's face and the grim expression he wore. Recognizing the near end of the man's patience, she hastened to get to the point.

"My son was making ready to leave, but was waylaid by a dispute between the blacksmith and the seneschal. He should arrive shortly."

At his silent stare, she gathered the rest of her courage and plunged into the depths of her plan, not stopping for air.

"In the last year, my son has rebuilt our home, 'tis far stronger now. The crops ... we've had a good harvest."

"And why I have chosen to gift it to de Chauret," the king said. "He has gone too long without reward. Merewood is now worthy of him."

She had expected his response. The Norman king had already divided up huge Saxon holdings and given them to many of his loyal followers. "But pray, bear with me a moment longer, Sire," she pleaded.

The hard glint in William's eyes softened slightly, and he nodded.

"'Tis under my son's direction and leadership that Merewood Keep has become wealthy again. Our people respect him. They would lay down their lives for him. Without him as their lord, our people would flounder. The harvests would suffer."

"Are you saying that Merewood's people would not tend to their fields and flocks if a Norman were their lord?"

Eyreka felt the blood drain from the top of her head to the pit of her stomach.

Before she could answer, he continued, "Do your people not realize that by the grace of God, and my word alone, they still live in a well-constructed keep and not buried beneath a pile of stones? I could have the head of each and every Saxon who dares to challenge my decree!"

Rumors had not exaggerated the power or temper of their new king. The threat issued was not idle and part of the reason for her bold plan.

Dizzy from the rush of blood to her feet and her king's words, she rasped, "Nay, Sire. 'Tis just that Garrick is heir to Merewood. It is in his blood. No one could possibly love the land more than he."

When the king continued to stare at her she added, "'Twould be to your advantage to ensure he remains as seneschal. He could continue to run things for Baron de Chauret, and our people would have immediate respect for him."

The king paused, stroking his chin. "Why would he stay on as less than master? What would he have to gain?"

Eyreka slowly closed the small gap that still separated her from the dais. A bead of sweat trickled down her back, while her mouth went dry. She had managed to get through the hardest part, laying out the reasons for her next suggestion. Trying to concentrate on the rest of her plan, and not how easily the man's hands would fit around her throat, she looked directly at her king and said, "I understand that Baron de Chauret is widowed."

"Aye. What of it?"

"My husband has been gone for three summers." Her stomach roiled and threatened to rebel. Had she eaten anything this morning, she would have surely lost it. "I would offer myself as wife to the baron. I am well respected as a healer and former mistress to our people."

She watched the expression in William's eyes go from surprise to calculating. "Mayhap 'twould bear consideration."

Now was the time to tell him. She had his full attention. If he refused, her sons need never know of her proposed bargain. No one need ever know. "As mistress, I could guarantee that my people would respect my new husband as lord. With my son running the estate, the revenues would not slacken, but continue to grow. All would profit from this arrangement."

William sat in silence, while she waited for him to deny or accept her request.

Finally he rose, nodded, and held out his arm. Lady Eyreka inclined her head and placed her hand on his forearm. He reached over and covered her hand with his. The familiar gesture made him seem less a king and more a man. It comforted her. If he could feel her trembling, he made no comment.

"Join me in the hall. I think de Chauret would do well to hear your proposal."

Eyreka drew strength from her king's strong grip. He had not shouted his displeasure at her bold suggestion. He had not had her clapped in irons and hauled away. She reached up and touched the base of her throat. Aye, she thought, still intact. All would be well. No one would have to leave Merewood. Odd, but she could almost feel his arrogant confidence suffusing her own doubt-ridden brain. Remarkably, her stomach calmed as he led her into supper.

"Augustin!" the king bellowed from the doorway.

"Aye," came the equally loud reply from across the wide expanse of the hall.

"Come and meet your bride," William commanded, "Lady Eyreka."

At the king's words, her heart skipped a beat. A hush immediately descended upon the crowded hall, servants and nobles alike falling silent, as they turned in unison to stare at her. The echo of booted footsteps filled the soundless void. The steps rang with confidence and determination as they drew ever closer. Then they stopped.

Eyreka's eyes widened as she stared up at the warrior standing before her. By Odin, he was large. His chest was broad and thick with muscle. When he reached out a hand to grasp that of his overlord, his tunic strained at the shoulders.

While the two men greeted one another, Eyreka took the opportunity to study the warrior, soon to be her husband by royal decree. His gray-streaked, chestnut hair was thick and wavy. Eyreka's hands tingled, remembering another man and another time, when she had plunged her fingers into his sun-kissed hair. Shaking herself free of Addison's memory, she let her gaze drift across Augustin's high cheekbones, the scar that arched across his chin, then on his eyes—his stormy-gray eyes!

The room spun wildly, while the floor swayed, and the walls closed in on her. He had Addison's eyes.

AUGUSTIN WATCHED THE hint of color drain from the woman's face and her eyes start to roll up in her head. He cursed as he swept her into his arms before she could slide to the floor in an unconscious heap. God made women beautiful and enticing, he thought to himself, to balance out the havoc they wreaked wherever they went.

Her breath blew out soft puffs of air against his neck, breaking his concentration. When he looked down at her, a long-dead emotion tried to make itself known, but he clamped it back into the small tidy corner of his heart that belonged always to his wife.

Still unconscious, she stirred in his arms and an uncomfortable awareness struggled to break free. Given her coloring, she was a Saxon. He would not deny that he had been attracted to her cool beauty, though it was the complete opposite of his wife's. Her white-blonde hair was streaked with strands of silver glistening in the torchlit room. Her pale skin looked as soft as silk. Though he may face the fires of eternity for it, he reached out hesitantly and ran his fingertip across her cheekbone down around the curve of her jaw and breathed in her sweet scent, a haunting combination of lavender and rain.

King William clapped a hand to Augustin's shoulder, breaking the spell she had unknowingly woven about him. "She's comely, old friend."

Shocked that he had let himself be attracted to the Saxon woman, Augustin ground out, "I do not need a wife." His teeth ached from clenching his jaw to keep from shouting the words.

"I say you do. Lady Eyreka has a sound plan that would not affect the revenues Merewood currently produces, even with the change in leadership." William's grip bit into the Baron's shoulder.

"I gave my word." De Chauret swore under his breath, thinking of Monique. Feeling trapped, no longer in control of the situation, he rasped, "I'll not marry again.

"And if I command you?" William's face began to mottle with rage.

Augustin recognized the look on his overlord's face and felt the heat of his own blood surge up his neck all the way to his forehead. He hung onto his temper. Never before had he refused a direct order from his liege. To do so now would not be wise. No doubt there would be another favored baron willing to wed the wealthy widow in order to gain control of her vast holding.

But to have to forsake his vow to Monique was akin to taking a blade through the heart. He could feel the open wound. He shifted the woman in his arms until her weight rested fully on his sword arm. Brushing a hand across his chest, he looked down, checking for blood.

There was none.

"Mayhap."

"'Aye' is the only response, my friend," William interrupted.

Augustin's grip tightened on Lady Eyreka while he stared at the man before him. They were equal in strength and stature, but he had not the power of a country behind him. Their conversation the day before now made sense. William was not looking for an estate to grant to him, he already had one picked out...and now a woman was part of the holding! Augustin's entire body stiffened, physically trying to hold out against what he must do.

Eyreka stirred, and her eyes shot open. She appeared disoriented. "Addison?" she whispered.

"Nay, milady, 'tis your betrothed, Augustin," the king answered.

The overwhelming urge to find this Addison and plow his fist into the man's face, whoever he was, caught Augustin by surprise, as did the unfamiliar jealousy snaking through him. Why should he care if another man's name came to those soft, rose-tinted lips?

"Please, release me." She squirmed in his embrace.

Her sudden, sharp intake of breath matched his own. When she shifted, she forced his grip higher on her rib cage. Her ice-blue eyes deepened to sapphire, transporting him back to another time and another woman. Her face blurred before his eyes, until she transformed into the form of his beloved wife. He wondered if Monique knew that her eyes gave away her thoughts.

The fog of memory cleared, revealing the Saxon woman once more. Momentarily confused, he wondered if it was the memory of his wife that called to him, or the woman in his arms? He ruthlessly pushed the disturbing questions aside and said, "I do not need a wife."

"You do." Eyreka's husky tones were echoed by the king's baritone.

"Come." William led the unlikely couple from the hall to his private chambers.

"I can walk."

Augustin refused with the shake of his head. At least in this he felt a small bit of control. Besides, he could not say why he refused to set the lady back on her own feet. Mayhap 'twas the fit. It had been a very long time since anyone felt so right in his arms.

Monique, his heart cried.

Is dead, his mind countered.

"I'll leave you to get acquainted." King William's gaze swept over the two. He chuckled softly before closing the door behind him. The king's amusement, coupled with Augustin's lack of control over the situation, started a slow burn in his gut.

The brief thought of his beloved wife was sobering. He set Eyreka on her feet, bracing a forearm behind her until she gained her balance.

"Thank you."

"Are you ill?"

"Nay," she said slowly.

"You swooned." He watched her closely for a reaction, a sign of guilt. Was it all part of her plan to lure him in, thinking she was weak?

"I am tired."

She swayed slightly and Augustin tightened his grip leading her over to a chair by the brazier. She would not look up at him, so he studied the top of her fair head. His mind raced, trying to find the words to convince her that he would never marry again. Before they parted company, she would understand that he would not be swayed by her obvious charms. If he could not find a way to convince William that he had to return to Normandy, to his family holding, then he would have to convince her that she did not want to marry him.

Just as he started to formulate a plan, Eyreka looked up at him, her eyes beseeching him. He stared back, focusing on her, as if seeing her for the first time.

Mon Dieu, she had Monique's ice-blue eyes.

His plans evaporated. He knew no matter what she asked of him, he would be powerless to say nay.

"Mayhap we could begin again, Baron de Chauret," Eyreka said softly. "I wish to tell you about my home."

CHAPTER TWO

"I'VE BEEN SUMMONED to meet with the king," Garrick announced to the guard standing outside his liege's chamber.

"He's meeting with an emissary from Merewood Keep," one of the men answered. "You'll have to wait."

Momentarily confused, and at a loss for words, Garrick stood and stared. He had not dispatched a messenger from the holding. Fragments of the last conversation he had with his mother slashed through him. She had planned this, he thought. She had extracted the details of the king's missive, remarkably showing little emotion over the possibility of losing their home. Stranger still, when he was making ready to leave, there had been a small war between their seneschal and the laborers. It was now suspect that his mother had not been available to step into the breach and handle the matter for him, as she was wont to do. Separately the events were puzzling, but when taken as a whole, the pieces fit together perfectly in the shape of a very familiar, meddlesome woman.

His mother, Lady Eyreka.

Garrick neared the wide doorway to the great hall. Though still daylight, twin torches flared and then hissed as he passed by them into the brightly lit room. The odor of herb-roasted venison and freshly baked bread filled his nostrils as he drew in a deep breath. He had the uncomfortably eerie feeling that he was being watched. Gradually, the room quieted. One by one, each and every person turned toward him and stared. He shifted uncomfortably from one foot to the other and ran a hand through his hair. He vowed not to give any of them the satisfaction of knowing how much he dreaded being the sole focus of so many Norman nobles.

He thought of his father and the housecarls who had followed him to their deaths in the Uprising, and the brave warriors who fought by his own side, trying to stem the flow of marauding Normans who had laid siege to his home. Each and every man who gave his life for the Saxon cause was worth three of the over-dressed, over-fed nobility who stood gaping at him.

He strode through the crowd, resolving to find his mother and meet with the king, only then could they begin the long journey home.

⫸⫷

"Merewood Keep is newly rebuilt," Eyreka began. "A curtain wall of stone ... acres of rich fertile soil, and a stream brimming with trout."

"Is the well within its walls?"

"Aye, and easily defended in times of siege."

"Is that a guess or do you know for a fact?" Augustin countered.

"The winter of 1044," she whispered, staring into the brazier, raptly watching the flames devour a piece of wood. Augustin paced before her, his thoughts churning around in time with the beat of his heavy footfall. He needed to know more before he spoke to his beloved daughter and his loyal men; they deserved more consideration than a mere moment of thought.

Augustin continued to pace. So, he thought, she is older than she appears. If the lady had married at three and ten, as was the custom, she could be older than him. He needed to carefully assess the situation at Merewood Keep.

"If you are widowed," he asked, "who is lord?"

He watched her eyes narrow, and he wondered if she would tell him the truth.

"My eldest son, Garrick, is lord and Jillian, his lady wife."

"Did he rebuild? Why is he lord?"

"My son is a fierce warrior of great reputation. When no one else could capture the traitor, Harald the Saxon, the Lord of Merewood did."

"Alive or dead?" Augustin prompted, his interest deepening.

"Alive." Her expression changed from uncertain to fiercely proud as she warmed to her story. "He and a small band of men rode into the rebel camp undetected and took them by surprise!"

"How so?"

"He drove a wagon filled with barrels into camp, supposedly containing the ransom demanded; only each barrel contained one of his warriors." She sat forward on the edge of the chair, waiting for his reaction.

Augustin smiled, knowing the value of employing surprise strategies, and nodded. "An impressive feat," he conceded, amazed that a young knight would use such a clever strategy. One he himself had not yet used.

"I understand that King William plans to ensure the entire border between Northumbria and Scotland is protected by Norman strongholds."

Augustin nodded. He knew the details of his king's plans, but was not going to enlighten her. Once the northern reaches of this isle were under William's rule, only the lands on the west coast, the land of the Cymry, the Welsh, would be left to be conquered. William's invasion had been brilliant. Even the Saxon Uprisings, just three years past, had been put down. Augustin did not doubt that the King of Scotland would pledge fealty to William.

"Are you ready to ride forth and claim Merewood as your new home?" she prodded.

Her direct gaze was starting to work its way under his skin. And like a sliver of wood, it annoyed him. "I need time to consider."

Should he accept her as wife? If he did, how would he break the news to his daughter? His daughter would balk at the thought of leaving London. He could not imagine her quietly accepting his marriage, having a new mother virtually thrust upon her. Augustin would have to carefully weigh the words he would use to sway his daughter and to graciously accept the king's offer. Though it galled him to have no say in the matter, Augustin would accept the Saxon woman as well.

His men should be pleased to have a safe haven, even if it was not their homeland, as he had promised. Angelique would simply have to adjust. Mayhap he would ask his young cousin to accompany his daughter on the journey north, or mayhap follow along at a later date.

The door to the chamber swung open, and the king strode into the charged silence. William stood feet apart, hands fisted on his hips and asked, "Well?"

"I have yet to convince him, milord," Eyreka said quietly. "I may need more time."

The king shook his head. "I have decided it is a sound plan."

Augustin could see the impatience his king held in check. Since William had already made up his mind, Augustin knew it would be useless to try to change it. "Aye, milord," he said through tightly clenched teeth. "I am truly grateful for the offer."

William reached out and patted him on the back. "I've already sent word to Merewood of my intention to install you as lord."

"But I—" Augustin felt the words stick in the back of his throat. The Saxon woman had planned this. It wasn't by chance as he had first thought. His direct look must have unnerved her. She flushed and refused to look him in the eye.

"I knew you would accept," William finished, with a look of smug satisfaction plastered on his face.

Augustin nodded. It would do no good to press the woman for the truth now. He would coax it from her later.

Augustin knelt before his overlord. "My thanks."

William nodded, waved him away and moved closer to Lady Eyreka, ignoring him completely. Augustin rose with a feeling of dread beginning to roil in his gut. His fate had been decreed as quickly as that. He would not be returning to Normandy. *Mon Dieu!* Had he been used? Was there a plot afoot to ensure that he never reached Merewood Keep alive? Because of his king, and the Saxon woman and her holding, he now had two battles to wage: one with his men and one with his daughter.

He paused a moment to consider his strategy. As far as his men were concerned, he knew they would accept his decision. He always encouraged his personal guard to voice their opinions. He smiled, anticipating their immediate reaction. They would grumble, argue, and challenge him, backing their words with physical rebuttal on the training field. Augustin looked forward to the discussion.

His smile turned into a frown, thinking of his daughter. If she reacted to the upcoming move the way he thought she would, it would be far preferable to deal with the physical abuse of his men than the razor-sharp edge of his darling daughter's tongue.

His decision made, he bowed to King William and Lady Eyreka then strode down the passageway toward the bailey, where he had left his men training.

Chapter Three

THE FORCE OF his opponent's blow reverberated up Augustin's arm, numbing it. The shocked surprise on the other knight's face must have mirrored on his own.

"Are you so eager for death?" the furious knight challenged. "Had we been in battle this day, you would have been hacked to bits, thrice over!"

Augustin accepted his cousin, Georges's words as the truth. His mind was not on the routine training drills, it was tangled up with the king's unwanted gift, and the dreaded discussion ahead of him.

"Henri," Georges, called out, "hand-to-hand!"

The older knight nodded his understanding and turned back to the men, shouting orders for them to pair up. Sounds of men engaged in combat rang out once again.

Suddenly exhausted, Augustin stood still as a stone while Georges helped remove the dented helm from his ringing head. Now that he was not moving, aches blossomed all over his body. Unfortunately, they were not painful enough to forget the upcoming confrontation with his daughter.

"She's going to hate me," Augustin said, holding his helm beneath his arm.

"She cannot," Georges said quietly.

The clash of steel upon steel lessened, dwindling until only the snort of the destriers, and heavy breathing of men, echoed through the sudden silence. The rest of his men must have sensed the seriousness of their discussion and paused to listen to their conversation.

He met his cousin's gaze and understood. They would speak privately later.

Augustin removed the heavy gauntlets and handed them to Georges. The ache behind his eyes intensified. Without thinking, he rubbed at it with grimy, sweat-slickened hands.

He swore ripely. The sweat and dirt he had unconsciously ground into his eyes stung.

"I don't know what to say to her," Augustin bit out, angry at his own indecision. He shifted the helm to carry it under his right arm and willed his left hip to loosen, so that he could walk with only the barest of limps.

Georges's eyes narrowed, and Augustin knew there was no hope his cousin hadn't noticed the old injury was bothering him.

"Did you at least try the remedy I left with you?"

"I do not need potions to make my body strong enough to fight. I can still best men half my age!" Augustin felt the boast stick in his throat when the muscles in his hip locked up and the familiar feeling of bone grinding against bone caused a shaft of pain to shoot into his lower back and down his leg.

Only his ironclad will kept him from pitching forward into the sandy dirt of the practice field. Sweat broke out all over his body as he struggled to stay upright.

Georges must have seen the look on his face because he grabbed at Augustin's arm to support him, making it look as if he was taunting him into testing his mettle further.

"I've got you," Georges ground out through clenched teeth. "Just a few more feet, and we'll be in the stable yard."

Augustin didn't dare open his mouth for fear the groan of agony he stifled would be ripped from him.

"Nod if you can make it that far."

The side of his head throbbed, but Augustin managed to nod.

The stable was nearly empty, with the exception of a few destriers and one of the stable lads filling the troughs with water from the well.

The cool, dark interior of the building blocked out the fierce heat of the sun, immediately chilling the sweat on his body.

"Milords." The young boy had stopped his chores, waiting for them to speak.

"Send for Baron de Chauret's squire," Georges ordered. "He is in the bailey tending to his master's horse."

"Aye, milord." The young lad answered, and ran off to do as he was bid.

"What can I do?" his cousin asked.

"I need to lie down flat so my hip will slip back into place," he answered.

"Here?"

"Aye," Augustin glanced around the still-empty stable. "The longer I wait, the harder it becomes."

Georges nodded his understanding and helped him to lie on the hard-packed dirt floor. The rich scent of it, combined with the familiar scent of hay and horse, soothed him.

He could feel his bones shifting again, but they didn't quite settle back into line. He would have to force the bones to realign themselves. It was sheer agony but he lifted his left leg, bending it at the knee, and brought it up to his chest. Breathing deeply, he lowered the knee toward the right side of his body. With a slip and a pop, his hip settled back into place.

Georges winced in reaction to the sound.

Augustin had seen his cousin hack through an entire company of men in the heat of battle. That the sound of bone sliding past bone should upset him was a surprise.

Their eyes met, and understanding flashed between them. It was not just the tie of blood that bound them together, they had been friends since fostering together during their tenth summer.

As if Georges could read Augustin's mind, he spoke softly, "'Tis not just the injury, 'tis the one who suffers from it." His gaze lingered on Augustin's face for a brief second before he reached out a hand to help him to his feet.

"Any warrior who can suffer through that can certainly brace himself to face his only daughter."

Augustin had to smile at that. "Mayhap now I will have the courage to do so."

Georges handed him back his helm, looking pointedly at the large dent in it. Augustin smiled and nodded his head. "But first, I'll have this pounded out."

⫸⫷

"BUT PAPA, I do not wish to leave London." The petite young beauty's voice was firm. Her ice-blue eyes had grown noticeably colder as they narrowed on him.

Augustin could all but feel the temperature drop in the chamber. "You may stay here until the holding is made ready for you."

"Papa," she pleaded, her eyes welling up with tears. Guilt swept up from his toes, settling in his gut. She was the image of her mother.

"You may stay here with cousin Genvieve, until I send for you."

"I will not leave," she announced, stamping her foot.

Augustin stopped in the doorway and turned around, "I had thought to let you ask whom you wished to accompany you on the journey, now..."

"I cannot leave."

"Angelique," Augustin sighed. "The king has decided to grant Merewood Keep to me. I would be ten times a fool to refuse him." He rubbed a hand across his throat. "I am rather fond of my head where it is," he finished grimly.

"Oh, Papa," Angelique cried, throwing herself into his arms. "I'm sorry."

As always, her tears cut right through his anger, humbling him. "Do not weep, *ma petite*," he whispered, absently smoothing the tangles from her midnight-colored hair. "'Twill be all right. We still have one another."

When her tear-stained face lifted, his heart clenched in his chest. She looked so like his beloved Monique that for a brief moment he actually considered defying his king. His head would not look so bad at the top of a pointed pike.

"Come. Let us find Genvieve, and ask if she would care to make the journey with you."

"I love you," Angelique whispered brokenly.

He gathered her into his arms and kissed the top of her head, "Not as much as I love you, *ma petite*."

CHAPTER FOUR

"MARRIED!" GARRICK BELLOWED.

"To whom?" Dunstan demanded, his frown as dark as his brother's.

Eyreka stared in disbelief at her outraged sons. If her youngest, Roderick, were here and not still in the Highlands with MacInness, he'd probably be standing with his brothers united in their opposition. Did they forget to whom they were speaking? By Odin, she was their mother! They should be showing her proper respect.

Indignation ignited her temper; it flared brightly. "'Tis not your place to question my actions," her throat was taut with the need to shout.

"His name, Mother," Dunstan said in a quiet voice.

She turned, hands on her hips, to glare at her middle son.

Barely able to hold back the verbal lashing poised on her tongue, she bit out, "You are not to speak of this. Understand?" They must know she was doing all that was in her power to save their home. Surely they realized that she dreaded suffering the Norman's touch.

Garrick reached out and grabbed hold of her arm. She shrugged it off and kept walking, refusing to let them see her fear. With each hour her fate drew closer, until she would be legally and honor bound to a Norman. May the gods help her, she had survived marriage to a Saxon, even learned to understand his Christian god. She had grown to love her first husband. But to have to do it all over again—when she had become so set in her ways, was worrisome—she did not know if she could.

A shiver of dread snaked up her spine. Chilled to the bone, she rubbed at the gooseflesh on her arms. Her steps faltered. Do not let it defeat you. Her husband's words echoed in her head. Drawing strength from them, she squared her shoulders and steadied her stride. As she rounded the turn in the passageway, she could hear the unmistakable sounds of more than one man's heavy footfall not far behind her.

Lord love them, they were as tenacious as their father and as single-minded as she.

"Mother!" Garrick called out to her.

"Wait!" Dunstan pleaded.

She slowed her steps and looked over her shoulder.

"I could force you to tell us." Garrick's voice sounded as bleak as the concern marring his brow.

"Mayhap."

"For the love of God!" Dunstan groaned, reminding her of her pledge to Addison to learn and then in turn teach their children all about the Christian god her husband prayed to. He had never insisted that she forget her own Viking upbringing or as he called them, her pagan gods. She taught her sons about their heritage, both Saxon and Viking. Her bloodlines traced back to the Viking rulers of old. They would no doubt understand just how upset she was by invoking Odin's name.

"Aye, and Odin," she answered. Not able to help herself, she reached out a hand and gently brushed the hard planes of Garrick's strongly chiseled jaw.

He closed his eyes and sighed.

"Mother—" Dunstan began.

She reached out and did the same to Dunstan. He, too, immediately quit his protests.

Love for her sons welled up within her, pushing her doubts

aside. She had made her choice and would not change her mind.

"Do either of you have any idea how very much I love the both of you?"

Garrick's sigh of exasperation was as loud as Dunstan's groan.

She knew she had their attention. "I would do anything to see that our home is not divided up and given away as gifts by our king."

Her eldest son's bellow was fierce, "You agreed to marry de Chauret?"

For once in his life, Dunstan was bereft of speech.

They had taken the news as well as she had expected them to. While her sons were still reeling from the news, she slipped away, knowing that they both needed time to grow accustomed to the idea. Not quite certain how long that would take, she decided it would be best not to appear for the midday meal. Her sons needed time to get used to the idea that she would marry again, and she had no desire to butt heads with their stubbornness again. Her head ached with the myriad of questions and problems that had arisen with the king's acceptance of her offer.

Walking back to her chamber she decided to order a bath and hopefully forget, at least for a short time, the anguished look in Garrick's eyes and the anger in Dunstan's. Drawing in a deep breath she knew it was time to prepare herself for the ceremony that would take place at sunset.

THE SOOTHING EFFECTS of her lavender-scented bath evaporated under the intense scrutiny of the nobles assembled to witness the marriage of one of their own to a Viking by birth, Saxon by marriage. She dared a glance at the two men standing near the far wall, and sighed. From their identically rigid postures, crossed arms, and set jaws, her sons were still angry for having been barred from her chamber earlier that afternoon.

She looked away, hoping that someday they would understand why she had taken matters into her own hands. Though the solution to her peoples' problem placed her right back where she did not want to be, dependent upon a man, she had had no choice. She glared at her future husband's guard; they all wore identical black expressions. Though none were as blatant, or as filled with contempt, as one of her future husband's vassals. The over-large, battle-scarred warrior with iron gray hair seemed to regard her as though she were a leper...unclean and unfit for the role she had bargained to fill.

The ceremony was blessedly brief, though still nigh impossible to remain standing when the quaking in her lower limbs threatened to topple her over. Fortunately, no one seemed to notice her discomfort, especially the quiet man who escorted her to the empty seat to the right of their king.

"Well done, Augustin." William thumped her husband on one of his broad shoulders. Eyreka flinched at the power behind the blow, but Augustin seemed not to notice. He was preoccupied, staring at the feast spread before them. He seemed enthralled. Her reaction was the opposite.

The amount of food was daunting, the display vulgar. When she thought of the poor souls that had nearly starved only a year ago, she rasped, "'Tis enough to feed Merewood's crofters for nigh onto a fortnight."

"I cannot imagine this fare would feed fifty of my men, let alone twice that number." Augustin looked at her for the first time since they had vowed to cleave to one another.

Taken aback, Eyreka shook her head. "Have you ever gone a day without food? Have you lain awake at night, your belly so empty that your mind is consumed with the worry that your family would starve before you could find a way to put a loaf of bread on the table?"

His gray eyes registered the shock her words must have given him, but his response was calm, "Aye. I have seen those that have suffered to the point they could not summon the strength to stand."

Surprise rippled through her at his words. He did understand. "I did not think—"

"Aye, you did not," he cut her off.

Before she could open her mouth to counter his words, his hand appeared before her lips, holding a plump piece of roasted fowl. "I am not hun—"

Her words were silenced by his strong fingers deftly placing the food between her lips. She could do naught but chew quickly and swallow. She planned to tell him she did not intend to remain silent while he criticized her in front of others. This time when she opened her mouth to speak, a hunk of bread soaked in the meat drippings was unceremoniously popped in.

If her new husband thought to fool those celebrating their union by solicitously feeding her the choicest bits of meat and broth-soaked bread, as was the custom for a newly married lord and lady, he was very mistaken. Theirs was a match made to benefit Merewood's people and the future of all of her sons.

When she tried to hasten her swallowing, to tell him just what she thought of his ploy to make everyone think theirs was a typical union, she choked. He whacked her between the shoulder blades and held a cup of spiced wine to her lips.

Furious at both his treatment of her and his total lack of attention, she grabbed his forearm.

That action stopped him cold. He paused in his conversation with the king and turned his glacial glare upon her. Undaunted, she started to speak. He made a move to feed her another bit of meat, but she forestalled his action with the sweep of her hand, knocking the meat out of his fingertips and into her goblet of wine.

"Mayhap you are not hungry?" he suggested in clipped tones.

"Had you let me speak earlier, you would know that I—"

He leaned close to her and whispered, "Mayhap you are eager to consummate our vows?" The low, seductive timbre of his voice sparked a familiar warmth deep within her. Captivated by the way his heated gray gaze raked her from head to toe, she was inexorably drawn to him, like the poor doomed moth drawn to candle flame. Eyreka shook her head to clear it, but she could not shake the image her mind had conjured up at his words. She did not want to be interested in her husband as a man, only as a figurehead to rule over her people, ensuring the stability of the home and her people's well-being.

The combination of unwanted desire and desolate sorrow warred within her breast, but she refused to let either emotion rule her actions. She had to be strong, to be smart, and do whatever she must to ensure Merewood's people would survive and flourish under Norman rule. Mayhap now was the time to catch him off guard and put her request to him. She placed a hand on his arm and leaned close.

His gaze snapped back to meet hers, but Eyreka was not to be put off by the temper she saw sparking there, "Aye, husband," she rasped, "I cannot wait to—" Before she could finish speaking, her words were cut off, as was her breath, when he grabbed her hand, pulled her to her feet and crushed her to his side.

"My liege," he said, not looking at her. "I beg your indulgence, but my wife ..."

King William looked up at Augustin and waved him away, his mouth already occupied, tearing the meat off of a haunch of venison.

Eyreka found that she had to run to keep up with her husband's furious stride. When he pulled her into his chamber, he turned back to bolt the door.

Her own anger abated when he turned around. It was then she noticed the taut line of his jaw. If he clenched it any tighter, she feared it would snap.

She took a step back.

He took a step closer.

She backed up another pace. Again he took a step closer. Finally, there were no more steps to be taken. She had backed her way across the width of the chamber and up against the edge of the bed.

He towered over her. Anger radiating from the powerful warrior she had wed caused a tingle of fear to trickle down her spine. This would not do at all. It had been necessary to get him alone, in order to convince him to hold off consummating their vows. Her plan was to get her new husband to agree to a marriage in name only. But one look at the virile warrior glaring at her, and she was afraid there would be no more talk this night. It was his right, but her plans to get him to agree to their union did not include intimacy.

She would make him see reason. Not knowing of any other way, she held a hand out to him, beseeching him to pause. "Milord, please?"

For an instant his eyes clouded with what she thought was confusion before they cleared. He took a step back and raked a hand through his hair, clearly as unsettled as she.

She saw her opportunity to speak and plunged ahead. "I wanted to speak to you earlier, but my messages were returned unopened."

He seemed confused, "What messages?"

"I sent my handmaiden to your chamber twice today with the message that I wished to speak to you, privately."

She noticed he was frowning when he turned away from her to stalk across the room. He clasped his hands behind his back and turned to walk back toward her.

Instead of offering an explanation, he asked yet another question. "What reason did she give for returning with the messages undelivered?"

"That you had not the time, nor the desire to speak with me." Her earlier anger at having her missive brushed aside returned. She tilted her chin up at a defiant angle and bravely met his gaze.

Instead of the convoluted reasons she thought he would use to try to excuse his behavior, he smiled.

She was appalled. "Do you mean to say that you actually left those instructions with the man guarding your chamber?"

He nodded, and she wondered had he spent so little time conversing with others and so much of it engaged in battle that he did not concern himself with the thoughts and feelings of others?

Her plans to secure a future for her sons was still just out of reach, and the dense warrior did not seem to be inclined to listen. Her cursed Viking temper, so like her father's, flared to life like a spark dropped onto a pile of dry twigs. She placed both hands against his rock-hard chest and shoved with all of her might. Completely taken by surprise, he faltered for a moment before losing his balance and crashing to the floor.

His eyes narrowed, and she made the mistake of looking away for an instant to gauge the distance to the door. Before she could take a step toward it, he grabbed her leg, tumbling her down into his lap.

"You have my undivided attention now, wife."

The husky sound of his voice unsettled her. She quickly wriggled off him and stood, and he made no move to stop her. Her body still trembled from the brief contact, unnerving her, while he seemed unaffected. Mayhap he had not felt anything when she'd landed on top of him. She frowned at the thought.

Smoothing her hands down the sides of her gown, she brushed away the tiny bits of rush that clung there. The small familiar motion helped give her time to compose herself.

His intense stare was unnerving, but she resolved to ignore it and convince him to agree with her plan. "I wish a boon."

If she thought to shock him, she failed miserably. He pushed up off of the floor in a fluid movement that bespoke his years as a warrior. He stood before her with his hands once more clasped behind him, his rigid control back in place.

Augustin's silence had begun to wear on her. He was obviously waiting for her to continue. Gathering all of her courage, she reached for the amber pendant hanging between her breasts. As soon as she touched it, raw power surged up her arm, strengthening her resolve. "I think that we should wait to consummate our marriage."

She paused, watching him closely to see if she could determine just what he was thinking. His face was devoid of all emotion ... completely blank. Eyreka suddenly felt sorry for any warrior who had to face her new husband's bleak countenance. It was distinctly unnerving, and he was not even armed!

She brushed that thought aside and said, "We need to accustom ourselves to one another. It would not do at all to arrive at Merewood out of sorts."

"And you feel that sealing our union would cause this discord?" The arch of his brow suggested he did not agree.

"Aye. Once we are more comfortable, and know one another better, then mayhap we can discuss this further."

Augustin was silent for the longest time. Not wishing to appear too anxious that he agree, Eyreka quietly studied him. It was then that she noticed that his eyes had dark circles of exhaustion surrounding them. Lines of worry marred his forehead, making him seem less the formidable adversary, more approachable.

Finally, when she could no longer stand the wait, she added softly, "I know that you had no desire to wed, but the people of Merewood should not have to suffer because our king deems it necessary to take away their lord. 'Twould truly be to your benefit to allow my son to stay on as seneschal and manage our holding until you are accustomed to our people."

The anger in his gaze dimmed. "And you would do anything for your people, would you not?"

Eyreka thought to disagree, but what would she have to gain by hiding the truth from him? Like it or not, she was now bound to him by her vow, freely given. "Anything."

Though she did not like the gleam in his eyes, she refused to weaken in her stance until he agreed.

"I will wait. Who knows, mayhap you will find that your people are more than willing to accept me as their lord."

And mayhap the Saxon people will rise up and overtake their

Norman oppressors. Eyreka doubted either event would ever come about. Though hopeful, she was realistic; it would take more than her marrying the Norman baron for her people to openly accept him as their lord.

CHAPTER FIVE

EYREKA WAS EXHAUSTED by the time she'd been roused and told to make ready for their journey back to Merewood Keep. Her husband had left their chamber after acquiescing to her request. She hadn't slept at all, wondering if he'd change his mind and storm back into their chamber.

They'd been riding since sunup and had just stopped to water the horses. A brief respite from their journey home, or so she thought, until one of her husband's guard spoke.

"To save time," Georges said, pacing in front of her, "I will tell you the rules."

"Rules?" Eyreka repeated slowly, focusing on the warrior. He had similar chiseled features and the same massive build as her husband, were they related? She knew so little about the baron.

"Aye," Henri echoed Georges's reply.

Her husband's vassals were glaring at her with nearly identical expressions of disdain.

"The first of which is never to question either Georges or myself," Henri stated in clipped tones.

"Why?" Eyreka's curiosity overrode her growing irritation.

Georges's expression darkened. He stopped pacing and strode over to where she sat on a fallen log. Henri moved to flank him, his expression equally dark.

Eyreka refused to let the men intimidate her. Years ago, as a new bride, she had been afraid to voice her own opinions. But she was no longer that same young girl; she was a woman secure in the knowledge that she had come up with a plan to change her sons' futures and had carried it through.

"Rule number two," Georges continued, as if she had not spoken. "All requests or problems should be brought to either Henri or myself. Augustin is far too busy—"

"I assure you," Eyreka interrupted, "I am very capable of solving problems that arise without any assistance or interference."

Henri and Georges stood red faced and speechless. Rather than ask what the rest of their rules were, Eyreka turned her back on them, needing to walk off her rising temper.

Halfway back to the stream, she heard the sound of a heavy footfall. Not ready to speak to any of the overbearing, arrogant Norman guard, she pretended not to notice the sound.

"Milady."

At the sound of her husband's deep baritone, Eyreka composed herself before turning around.

"Aye?" She stopped and waited for him to catch up.

"Georges said there is a problem."

Eyreka snorted, "There most definitely is." She watched his posture stiffen, as if preparing himself to hear something distasteful.

He grasped his hands behind his back and waited for her to speak.

"I have no intention of following anyone's rules ever again."

"Rules?" he asked softly, "What rules?"

"Yours," she spat out. The mere thought of reporting to the two odious vassals, who clearly had no liking for her, added to her worry that mayhap her plans would not work out smoothly.

"I do not have any rules—" he began, and then stopped. "Oh, I see."

"Do you? That will make our transition much smoother. It is necessary for you to understand at the outset that I am used to running the keep. As mistress, I take orders from no man."

Augustin's eyes darkened to the color of summer storm clouds. "'Tis past time for us to reach an understanding, lady."

Augustin's tone sounded harsh … controlled. "I intend to run this holding as I see fit. As such, you will do as I say, when I say, without question."

Eyreka could not say if it was her husband's attitude, or his ill-mannered vassals' treatment of her, but it pushed her over the edge. Blinded by the force of her anger, she jerked her knee up and jabbed out with her left fist simultaneously, just as her father had taught her years ago before he went on one of his raids.

Augustin's grunt of surprise was followed by a moan of anguish. He doubled over, trying to catch his breath.

Eyreka could not hold back her smile. Her arrogant warrior husband may be larger and stronger, but she had the power of knowledge on her side. Cunning and knowledge could best size and strength, if used wisely.

She knew that her aim had been true. Every man had the same weakness; the trick was catching that weakness just so.

"I take orders from no man." She turned on her heel and walked back over to where she had tethered her horse. Surprised that she could no longer see her shadow, she looked up. Ominous dark clouds blocked out the sun.

The huge black beast still munched contentedly on sweet meadow grass where she had left him. She absently ran her hand along the beast's velvety-soft muzzle. Her mount blew out a puff of warm, moist air and nudged her until she pet him again. The first drop of rain hit her on the tip of her nose.

"Are all men so thick-headed?"

Her horse whickered, nodding his head up and down.

"Do tell," she said with a smile.

Two hours later, soaked to the skin, she was no longer smiling. The storm had caught them unawares. The road ahead lay in darkness. Every other heartbeat, bright-white flashes split the angry sky.

AUGUSTIN CURSED HIS king and the storm; because of the first, he was caught in the second.

He pulled his woolen cloak tighter to his soaked torso, trying to trap some of his body heat, before it too escaped as fine mist in the air.

The day had started where the night had ended; he was at odds with his wife. The woman had gotten past his guard and landed that ego-shattering blow. Why had he let her walk away? They had not spoken since. He already knew she would do anything to help her people. Now he amended that to include getting her own way, using her cunning wit, small fists, and bony knee. Eyes narrowed, he conceded the first battle was hers, but the next one would be his.

The journey to his new home would take them seven days north of London ... under normal conditions. Lifting his face to the lashing rain, he was afraid the fierce storm would add two or three more days.

He wiped the rain out of his eyes. A gust of wind lifted the edges of his cloak, leaving his side unprotected. The second gust left him rain-soaked and colder. He glanced back over his shoulder to where his wife rode, surrounded by his guard. The small party fared no better than he.

A flash outlined her slight form for a brief second. She still rode with her face forward and her jaw set, uncomplaining, as she had for the last few hours. She was definitely unlike any other female he had ever encountered. He had ridden with the king's royal party on more than one occasion and had had to listen to numerous female complaints.

"She looks frail," he grumbled, to no one in particular.

"But she's still in the saddle," Georges replied.

Before he could think of a retort, a brilliant blue-white fork of lightning struck a nearby tree and blew it apart. The explosion shook the very ground on which they rode.

As he heard a horse's whinny of fright behind him, Augustin's horse tried to bolt, but he controlled the huge black beast with a few harsh commands and the strength of his muscular thighs. By the time he had his own mount back under control, his wife's mount was standing on its hind legs, frantically pawing the air in front of it. The storm had spooked her horse. He tugged on the reins of his destrier and rode toward her.

"By the breath of Odin," he heard her cry out.

"*Mon Dieu!*" Augustin made a grab for her horse's halter, but his grip slid off the rain-drenched leather. In the split-second it took to try again, another crack of thunder sounded nearby.

A flash of lightning lit the sky, illuminating the road ahead. He watched his wife's hands pull back hard on the reins, and the horse rear up once more. The sudden darkness that followed filled his heart with dread. When the next flash of light framed horse and rider, his gut clenched.

He knew he would be too late.

The echoing thunder boomed loudly, covering the twin shrieks of terror made by woman and horse. The sudden stillness that followed cut through him like a hot knife through butter.

He leaped off his horse and ran, the next flash showing what he had feared. No sign of Eyreka's horse, and a dark form lying in the road.

"Eyreka," he rasped, kneeling beside her in the mud. Mixed feelings raged through him. Concern tangled with the need to protect, while a persistent voice urged him to gloat over her misfortune. Although she had bested him earlier, he did not feel an ounce of satisfaction. Concern lanced through him.

When she moaned, he commanded her to lie still. With a deft touch, he checked her limbs for signs of a break. His fingers were far from steady as he pressed on her left ankle. Her sharply in-drawn breath made him pause, then she stiffened beneath his probing.

"Here?" he asked, gentling his touch.

"Aye."

She bit her bottom lip. He knew she was in pain, but trying to hide it from him.

"Can you walk?" Augustin wanted to see just how far she would go to be accommodating.

Her eyes, dulled with pain, met his, alert and searching. "I think so."

Augustin placed his hands around her waist, and pulled her to her feet. He was amazed that she even tried to stand. Any one of the score of women he knew would have swooned by now, or at the very least given in to tears.

His lady wife held onto his forearm with a death grip, putting more of her weight on the injured ankle. Another sharp intake of breath told him all that he needed to know. It was either badly sprained or broken. A sudden burst of pride filled him, taking him by surprise at the realization that his wife had the makings of a warrior. Why that should make him feel proud of her, he could not answer. He wanted to feel nothing for her. She was a means to an end, necessary to the new plans he now had for his daughter's future.

Before he could tell himself he had no time for these feelings, or a wife, Eyreka let go of his arm. She stood with her chin up and eyes blazing with what Augustin could recognize as a combination of fierce pride and grim determination. The unwanted feelings that had surged through him earlier came back. *Mon Dieu*, she was a woman a man could be proud of.

Eyreka took a halting step before he reached out and grabbed her upper arm. The small, but firm muscle beneath the cloth sleeve surprised him. He had not noticed it the night before. His gaze snapped back to her face.

His thought must have registered on his face, because she spat out, "I am not weak."

For a moment, rain blurred his vision, and his dead wife's face was superimposed over Eyreka's. Who was this woman? He blinked, and once again he saw Eyreka. My wife in name alone. If she were to be believed, in order to maintain a peaceful existence, he would have to make certain that they continued to live separate lives.

Georges spoke from behind him, "She reminds you of someone?"

"Nay," he answered, but his cousin had already moved forward to help his new mistress around a mud puddle, over to the hastily prepared shelter he and the others were just completing. It was not much, but mayhap the tightly woven lengths of linen stretched between the leafy canopy of two trees would shed enough water so they would be a bit drier than they would have been without it.

Augustin looked at the hastily constructed shelter and thought how easy it would be to tear it apart. It reminded him of the haste with which he married the widowed Saxon woman, and how easily it could all come undone if he did not uncover the truth behind his wife's actions. He did not trust easily.

In the meantime, it would be best if he strove to seek a peaceful coexistence with his Saxon bride. She could be the making, or the undoing, of his life at Merewood Keep. Though he did not trust her, he would have to try to get along with her. Mayhap in time, he would see beyond the shield of pride she hid behind.

His daughter's expressive face suddenly filled his thoughts. She was so very unhappy at the prospect of leaving the very active life she led at court to travel to—what she would no doubt deem to be—the very fringes of the civilized world.

While he wanted his daughter to be happy, he could not condone giving in to her latest whim, allowing her to remain in London. If she were to be married in a few years, she would need to learn to obey, or at least learn to be accommodating. Under his new wife's tutelage, mayhap his daughter could learn much more than how to manage a household and direct the great number of servants necessary to run such a household. Lady Eyreka claimed to be a great healer, mayhap his daughter would learn the many uses of herbs that could be grown in the keep's garden.

He could no longer put off the inevitable, though his daughter be of an age where it would be expected that he arrange a suitable marriage for her, he did not want to have to find Angelique a suitable husband. The very thought of his daughter betrothed in two years and married by the age of four and ten did not sit well. *Merde!* She was still a young girl ... mayhap he would be better off sending her to a convent, rather than bringing her into the middle of such a volatile situation as the incoming unwanted Norman lord over a holding full of Saxon warriors, ruling over Saxon crofters, who were bound to resent his presence.

He shook his head. It was better to have his new wife train his daughter and see her every day, than to have her locked away in a convent. Augustin could not think of a household he would want to send her to in this country, had they been in Normandy ... He truly dreaded the task ahead of him. Angelique was bound to pitch a fit, demanding to choose her own husband.

Thoughts of seeing her wed reminded him of his lovely Monique. Had she truly been of the same age when he had married her? Why did no one warn him that a father would not wish to part with his only daughter when the time came to do so? If only Monique were still alive, she would have prepared him for this day and would have been there to share in their daughter's marriage. His hands clenched as anger churned through him. They should have had their whole lives to share their love. Raw anguish ate at his gut like a hungry wolf tearing at its latest kill.

"Augustin!"

Georges's shout from beneath the makeshift cover forced him to return to the present. He strode through the ankle-deep mud puddle that nearly spanned the entire road. Judging from the ominous looks on the faces of his men, it would be a long, wet night.

BARGAINING WITH THE LADY OF MEREWOOD

THE RAIN LESSENED sometime during the night, but continued throughout the next few days. By the time the sun finally made an appearance, midway through their fourth day of travel, there was not an inch of their party, or the road they traveled, that was not wet and muddy.

"I'd rather walk."

"Milord has decreed that you shall be carried or ride, not walk." Henri's voice cracked with anger.

"I do not care what milord has decreed." Eyreka nearly bit her tongue, holding back a scream of frustration at the gray-haired bull of a man who tried to wrestle her from the saddle.

A dark and dangerous expression settled on Henri's harsh features. For a brief moment, Eyreka regretted angering the warrior. But it could not be helped; she would simply not accept any assistance while she was looking for a private place to relieve herself.

Lord, but the man was stubborn, insisting on trying to help, while she was just as insistent that she needed none. Finally, she ended the wrestling match with a well-placed boot to the middle of Henri's broad chest.

To her utter shock, and the warrior's, he lost his footing. For a moment in time, he was tipped back on his heels, hands waving to steady himself. She found her first smile in days, as the warrior fell backward landing with a splat in the thick black muck that surrounded them.

Eyreka threw her head back and laughed until her sides ached. Henri de Beoudine reminded her of the last time the swinekeep's very large pig raided her vegetable gardens at Merewood. The warrior was thrashing about wildly and making a horrible racket, very like that same pig.

When she caught her breath, she saw her husband out of the corner of her eye. His countenance was as dark as the ever-present storm clouds following them.

As he strode forward, looking neither to the left nor right, she unconsciously grabbed hold of the amber pendant she wore, ignoring Jillian's warnings to be careful what she wished for while holding the bit of amber, and wondered what would happen if he...

"Milord!" Jean and Jacques shouted as Augustin slipped and went down into the same puddle of muck as Henri.

Eyreka burst into peals of laughter, she'd gotten what she'd wished for. The two fierce-looking Norman warriors were tangled together in a mass of thick black muck and legs. When she dared a look over to where the rest of the men stood waiting, she instantly sobered.

Every one of her husband's men were standing with their feet apart, hands clasped behind their backs, glaring daggers at her. Well, she thought, she had certainly done it this time. Not only was Henri mad at her but her husband and every one of his men, as well. But she had faced a similar foreboding group men last year after she and Jillian had been liberated from the hands of their rebel captors. If she could face Garrick's intimidating vassal, Winslow MacInness, and the O'Malleys—his group of Irish mercenaries, she could handle the angry-looking group standing before her now.

Hoping to break the tension, she called out, "Georges, I believe my husband requires assistance... and a bath," she added under her breath.

Augustin stared coldly at her, but said nothing as he stalked to the stream that ran alongside the road. Looking up at the midday sun, she knew it would be hot enough to wash away the mud that was caked to their travel-worn clothing and have their things dry by sundown.

The youngest of the guards, Aimory de Noir, stood next to her mount with a smile twitching at his lips.

"You dare to laugh at my husband?"

He immediately sobered and averted his gaze. "Nay, milady."

She laid a hand on his arm. "I will not tell anyone." His gaze met hers, gratitude and understanding shining in his warm brown eyes. "Would you help me down?" she asked, "I need to have a moment of privacy."

Aimory lifted her from the saddle and helped her walk to a thick stand of trees, then turned his back and walked a short distance away. Finally, she would have her privacy. Mayhap she had even found a friend among the austere Norman guard. Eyreka had a feeling it would be a blessing in the next few days ahead.

CHAPTER SIX

As she had feared, the remainder of the journey homeward was difficult. Her husband's men were openly hostile toward her whenever she was left alone with them, with one exception, Aimory.

She glanced to her right, where the loyal warrior rode, and had been riding for the last few days. He smiled when their eyes met, and she noticed a deep dimple on one side of his mouth. Eyreka sighed; he was so like her youngest son, Roderick. She missed him terribly and wondered how much longer it would be before word reached them from the Highlands. He had already been gone three months without a word, and she was ready to send Garrick and Dunstan out in search of their brother.

Aimory said something and was obviously waiting for her to reply. She smiled, "I am afraid I was woolgathering."

"It won't be long until we reach Merewood, milady." Aimory hesitantly smiled.

Her husband's youngest knight was a good man, she thought. He had not joined in when the others each took a turn listing the rules she would have to follow while under their protection.

"Rules," she muttered.

"Mistress?" Aimory paused, as if waiting for her to continue.

She met his gaze and mumbled a foul word under her breath.

"I trust you do not truly wish it to be so." The sound of her husband's gruff voice surprised a gasp from her. He reined in his horse alongside of her. His direct look had her blushing to the roots of her white-blonde hair. He had heard what had not been meant for anyone's ears.

She rasped out, "My apologies, milord."

Hoping he would understand her need to regain her composure, she let her gaze sweep the woods that lined the road. The trees were lush with new growth. Supple green leaves seemed to have doubled in size overnight, now that the early summer sun arrived to dry out the rain-drenched countryside.

One of the warriors called out from up ahead, "Merewood Keep looms on the next rise."

Eyreka gave a swift nudge with her heels, to urge her horse from a canter to a gallop. The rain-washed air rushed past her, filling her with elation as she gained the crest of the rise. She did not stop to take in the beauty of the land; she knew it well. Aye, she'd seen it with her eyes closed, as she lay dreaming of the day she would return triumphant in her quest.

Hooves thundered alongside of her. She did not need to turn her head to see who rode to catch up to her. Her heart knew her husband would be anxious to ride alongside of her through the gates of her home, nay she qualified, their home. A feeling of uneasiness swirled around her, making her question all that she had done. The low-pitched grumbling coming from behind them had her wondering if their two peoples would be able to meld their lives together, or if they would merely tolerate one another's existence?

She glanced at the man beside her. Would her sons come to respect the man she had wed? A frisson of uneasiness filled her. Would Augustin seek her out, longing to confide in her at the end of their weary days? His now-familiar scent, a combination of body-warmed leather and man, swept past her making her wonder if there would come a time when he would demand his husbandly rights … no matter what they had agreed to.

"Give the sign." The command in her husband's voice jarred

her out of her reverie. He would not countenance a refusal on her part and was correct in his assumption that she would do as he asked without question.

She inclined her head and raised her right hand in the air, fisted it, then brought it down to her heart, but the host of warriors lining the walkway atop the curtain wall remained standing with arrows notched, battle-ready even after she called out, "Patrick!"

The largest warrior nodded his head, and as one, the guard finally relaxed their stance, but not their arrows.

"Welcome home, Lady Eyreka," the redheaded giant shouted in reply.

Unnatural quiet descended upon the two groups of warriors. By Odin! Did her son's thick-headed guard have to show their disapproval of the new lord so blatantly? By all rights, the Saxons guarding the holding should have lowered their weapons. Had they brains the size of a flea with so little regard for their heads? The slight to the new Norman lord was received with stony silence.

But she had envisioned such a greeting upon her return and was prepared to circumvent it. "Patrick, gather your men in the great hall within the hour. I wish to introduce my new husband."

Whatever the reaction she expected from the Irish mercenary, open-mouthed shock was not one of them. In an attempt to get his attention, she gave him yet another task. One guaranteed to get him moving.

"I want you to personally see to Lord Augustin's destrier, have Kelly see to mine." She softened her command with an encouraging smile.

Patrick looked as if he had swallowed a hot coal from the brazier. His entire face flushed red, with what she knew was anger, but the man did not disappoint her. Though the task usually fell to one of the stable lads, to curry and feed the lord's horses, she knew the warrior would do her bidding. From the look on his face, the young warrior knew he had been in the wrong. She could sense Patrick also realized it would have displeased her son, Patrick's overlord. Something not one of Garrick's men would do.

"As you wish, milady," he answered through tightly clenched teeth. Signaling for the hefty wooden bar securing the gate to be lifted, the gate swung open, and the Norman party entered.

Augustin seemed to watch the by-play with interest, but as yet held his own council. He dismounted and handed the reins to the red-faced warrior with but a glance in the man's direction, then strode to where Eyreka sat atop her own mount.

"Lady wife," he said holding out his hands and grasping her about the waist, but instead of setting her on her feet, he swept her into his arms and stalked toward the hall. Her brain ceased to function as his warmth and strength surrounded her.

"Put me down," she commanded.

"Nay," he answered, a false look of contentment plastered upon his face.

"I am perfectly able to walk the short distance to the hall," she insisted.

"Aye, but I do not have all afternoon to wait for you to accomplish such a feat with your injured ankle."

Eyreka gave up trying to reason with the stubborn man and looked over his shoulder for help. The look on the faces of her son's guard was murderous, and each and every one had a hand on the hilt of their broadswords.

"Best make it look as if you are enjoying my attentions, wife," Augustin warned. "The keep's guard appear eager for spilled blood—mine."

Eyreka forced herself to smile. Her son's household guard silently challenged her husband's, who appeared more than ready to answer in kind. She and Augustin were literally surrounded by two hostile groups of warriors poised for battle. What a foolish, stubborn lot warriors were. It would be up to her to ease the tension. No one appeared ready to back down.

She stroked the back of her hand lightly against her husband's cheek. He faltered in his step, and pinned her with his stormy-gray gaze. She stroked his face again.

"What are you about, wife?" he rasped in her ear.

"I am merely showing you that I am enjoying your attentions. Otherwise, the guard may get the wrong idea."

He tightened his grip; his fingers biting into her arm.

"Your grip belies the look of contentment you show our people, husband."

Augustin relaxed his grip, as he took the steps up into the hall two at a time. Her serving maid was waiting with a tray piled with trenchers made of brown bread. The yeasty scent was a welcome diversion to the tension that clogged the air of the bailey.

She smiled at the maidservant, "Sara, please send for Jillian."

Her husband moved to set her gently down upon a chair.

"Milord, I would prefer to wash away the dust of our journey before I join you."

He straightened back up and gathered her close, "As you wish." They followed Sara out of the hall to the stairs leading to the second level and the privacy of the solar.

"I trust your serving maid is capable of assisting in your bath, wife?"

The deep timbre of his voice did not match the hard look in his eyes. When he set her on a chair, a chill swept over her. He had not willingly touched her since the night they wed. His penetrating gaze made her stomach flip, and the words catch in her throat, finally she managed to nod in agreement.

"I leave you then to make myself presentable to greet our people." He bowed and followed one of the servants to the bathing chamber.

"DOES IT PAIN you, milady?" Sara asked, helping Eyreka from the wooden tub.

"Only when I walk." Eyreka gritted her teeth against the pain, thankful she did not have to hide her feelings from her maid.

"Then you should remain up here in bed," Sara suggested, wrapping the drying cloth about her.

"Nay, I must introduce Lord Augustin to our people. To wait might give them the idea that he is of no consequence." Eyreka braced herself to put a bit of her weight on the injured ankle and raised her arms above her head.

"Is he, then?" the young woman asked, helping her mistress put on a clean chainse.

Once the under-tunic was in place, Eyreka answered, "He is my husband. As such, he will rule our home, listen to grievances, and settle disputes."

"You accept him readily?" Sara asked, smoothing the soft woolen folds of the dark-blue bliaut into place.

Eyreka's heart beat faster, as her serving maid's words took hold. "Aye," she half-lied. No one need ever know theirs was to be a marriage in name only. A frisson of unease swept through her, knowing that living in the close confines of Merewood Keep, very soon one and all would be aware of the lord and lady's affairs. The servants and their people's livelihoods depended largely upon the lord's mood. It would be to her peoples' benefit to know as much as possible about their new lord's likes and dislikes, learning his moods and preferences would be expected. She had done the same, learning to get along with her first husband and his people all those years ago. It had served her well. It would serve her people well.

"'Twill be a sound start to your marriage then, Reka," Jillian said, entering the room, distracting her from thoughts of living in one another's pockets and the possibility of suffering from the slings and arrows of misplaced gossip.

"Jillian," Eyreka greeted the daughter of her heart with a warm hug.

"And where is my darling grandson?" she asked, trying to

divert the conversation away from her unexpected marriage back to safer ground.

"Asleep, praise the Lord." Jillian sighed, helping Eyreka to sit with her leg propped up on a wooden stool. "Garrick did not ride with you?" Jillian asked, settling into the opposite chair.

"My son was too overcome with joy now that I have taken a husband." Eyreka absently rubbed her fingertips along the arm of the chair.

"Mayhap he is still trying to rein in his fierce Viking temper."

Eyreka could not lie to Jillian. "He and Dunstan were incensed. They did not agree with my decision to marry Augustin."

"Had you sought their opinion prior to the marriage?"

Eyreka could feel the heat of her anger starting to build, but she suppressed it. She did not want to be angry with Jillian. "My sons have no say as to the course of my life."

"Mayhap another solution could have been found—" Jillian began.

"There was no other way. The king was going to grant the land to de Chauret, with or without me as his bride. How could I take the chance that de Chauret would marry one of his own people? How could I risk our servants being replaced one by one, while more and more Norman servants were brought in? Would you have me go out on horseback and greet each and every one of our crofters in their fields and homes to tell them they were to be put off land their fathers and their father's fathers had planted and reaped for the last hundred years?"

Jillian took Eyreka's hands in her own and squeezed them. "Best not to keep our new lord waiting. He asked that I find out if you were ready."

"Aye," she answered, rising awkwardly from the chair.

"Allow me, wife."

Augustin must have been waiting outside her chamber door. He crossed the room and deftly swept her into his arms. Though she tried hard to ignore the feeling, she tingled from the top of her head to the soles of her feet. Her husband's actions continued to confuse her. He was at once solicitous and arrogant, unfeeling and compassionate. He was a hard man to comprehend and impossible to ignore. She bit back the sigh of pleasure she felt being held in his capable arms.

She stole a look at him through her lowered lashes to try to discern what he was thinking. His jaw was clamped so tightly, that a tiny muscle pulsed in time with his footsteps. His long strides were smooth, never jarring her, as they descended the stairs to the crowd waiting below.

Eyreka sensed the tension vibrating in her husband. Knowing he would be focused on the coming meeting, she silently agreed that he would do well to be wary among her people, nay, she thought, our people. She hoped that they would accept him in time. Mayhap they would, if she were very careful to show him the respect that the lord of the keep was due. Whether or not he was deserving of it, only time would tell.

CHAPTER SEVEN

THE HALL WAS filled to bursting. Augustin's personal guard sat on one side of the long oaken table, while some of Garrick's men sat on the other. Eyreka felt all eyes turn toward them as Augustin carried her into the room.

Patrick rose from his seat and walked over to the doorway. "Is there a reason then that you cannot walk, Eyreka?"

Augustin's face darkened at the younger knight's words. "You will address my wife as milady," he commanded from between clenched teeth.

Eyreka laid a hand on her husband's arm in an effort to stem his rising anger. "Patrick is one of my son's vassals, second in command only to Winslow the Scot. As such, I have given him permission to address me as Eyreka."

Her husband stiffened, as if he had been dealt a harsh blow. "As you wish, lady wife."

It was then she realized that she had not yet given Augustin leave to address her as Eyreka. She tilted her head and stared at the chiseled profile that was so close to her own. Would he even wish to become that friendly with her? Would she want him to?

Knowing Patrick would not be satisfied until she'd answered, him she said, "I had a slight mishap and injured my ankle."

"Be that as it may," Augustin continued as if she had not spoken to the younger man, "when we are among our people, he must address you as befits your position as my wife, lady of this keep."

Eyreka did not wish to argue in front of her people, nor did she want to add fuel to his growing anger. She nodded her head in agreement and noted he seemed satisfied. Augustin started walking toward the seats left vacant in the middle of the long table.

Though she knew he was angry, he gently settled her in the chair and placed a hand upon her shoulder. Eyreka felt it was her place to make the introductions, but as she opened her mouth to speak, Augustin cut her off with a direct look.

"By now most of you have heard that King William has chosen me as the new Lord of Merewood Keep." He paused for a moment before continuing. "As such, I intend to assume my duties at once. While I have spent most of my time on the fields of battle, I am not ignorant of the duties a lord has to his people. As such, I will begin by hearing minor grievances tomorrow, after Lady Eyreka and I break our fast."

With that, he sat down and motioned for one of the pages to fill his goblet. The boy approached with two pitchers.

"Our harvest was plentiful," Eyreka said smiling. She was very proud of her son's accomplishments. "We have the finest mead and wine to offer, milord."

Eyreka motioned for the page to fill her goblet with mead. She turned and offered it to Augustin. "Taste mine. See if it is to your liking."

Her husband's smoke-colored eyes visibly darkened at her words. His strong fingers brushed against hers, as he accepted the goblet. Eyreka feared he had misunderstood her meaning, reading more into her words than she intended. His steely gray gaze penetrated the mask of contentment she wore, stripping away layer upon layer of the false happiness she strove so hard to weave about herself, until her own turbulent emotions were left raw and exposed.

Eyreka thought she should explain herself, and try to undo

the damage she had already done by letting the man she married see the glimpse of the passion she had only shown one man before him.

"I'll have the mead," his voice rumbled from deep within his massive chest.

The page poured another goblet and moved on down the table filling the empty cups. The movement broke the powerful hold Augustin seemed to have over her.

Patrick sat quietly on her right, his brooding presence becoming more and more difficult to ignore. While her husband was busy filling their shared trencher with bits of meat and cheese, she turned to the warrior and spoke in hushed tones.

"What is it you wish to ask?"

"I would hear then why he carries you about as if you are unable to walk on your own two feet."

"I was thrown from my horse when—"

"Thrown? Do you think me daft? There's not a horse for miles around that would dare," Patrick said with a grin.

Eyreka could feel herself flush with embarrassment at the younger man's praise. "I was riding an unfamiliar mount in the middle of a fierce storm."

"If the storm was so fierce, why were you riding at all?" Patrick's voice hardened.

"Because my lady wife is intelligent enough to do as she is bid," Augustin answered for her.

Eyreka could feel the flames of her temper begin to flare. If she were not careful to control her anger, it would blaze out of control. She swallowed the rejoinder that lay poised upon her tongue and answered evenly. "As often as possible, milord."

Patrick's eyes showed his disbelief, while the look in Augustin's suggested he too doubted her softly spoken words. Striving not to lose her temper, and maintain a calm facade for her people's sake would be difficult enough. But it would surely be a trial to finish the meal without hitting either man over the head with her goblet. She groaned inwardly; the provocation was sure to be great.

At last the interminable meal ended. Without thinking, Eyreka started to push herself out of her chair. Dagger-sharp pain slashed through her ankle the moment she put her weight on it. While she tried to catch her breath, her ankle folded beneath her.

"Eyreka!" Augustin called out, steadying her, letting her lean on him.

Concentrating on controlling the pain that brought tears to her eyes, she wondered if she imagined the concern in Augustin's voice. Her hands were not steady as she brushed the tears from her eyes. A pox upon that horse ... and another upon her ankle for making her an invalid.

"Easy, milady," Patrick said, taking hold of her other hand. "Kelly!" he called to the warrior standing by the doorway.

"Aye?" The warrior walked over to where Eyreka sat, now cradled in her husband's arms.

"Lady Eyreka has injured her ankle," Patrick said. "Can you have a look at it?"

Eyreka saw her husband hesitate and start to open his mouth. She quickly explained, "Kelly is a gifted healer, as well as a powerful warrior."

Augustin inclined his head.

Kelly knelt before her, closed his eyes and carefully prodded the bones of her foot. He sighed and opened his eyes. "'Tis badly wrenched, but the bones feel intact."

Eyreka had not thought it was broken, but was relieved to hear another healer proclaim it so. Unfortunately, the throbbing pain would not be ignored for long; it had slowly built in intensity while they ate.

"She could have reinjured it just now," Kelly added. "You should stay off your feet for a fortnight ... rest your ankle on a pillow ... mayhap two. I'll have Sara mix up a batch of your comfrey root concoction for a poultice, milady."

"Thank you, Kelly." Eyreka tried to smile, but could not quite pull it off. "That should help with the swelling."

"Come, lady wife, 'tis past time for you to retire."

Eyreka's heart fluttered at the thought of spending the night in the same chamber as her husband. She had not thought far enough ahead to discuss their sleeping arrangements once they reached Merewood. She was no newly married maid, unaware of what transpired between man and wife—but he was not Addison—he was Augustin, her husband in name only. It would not do to forget their bargain, no matter how her traitorous body reacted to his voice or his solicitous touch.

"I am tired," she whispered, as they reached her chamber.

"Leave us."

The young servant waiting in their chamber hesitated. "But milady—"

"I will see to my wife."

The maidservant made a hasty retreat.

Her gaze darted from the closing door to her husband's impassive face. He seemed too relaxed to her, belying the banked embers flaring to life in his dark gray eyes. She was trapped by her unwanted reaction to the man she had pledged her life to. But she had no intention of sealing that pledge. At least not yet.

"My every need?" she asked, before she was able to stop herself.

"All that is in my power to fulfill." His gray eyes betrayed his desire-laced frustration.

"Do you go back on your word, husband?"

"Why do you ask?"

"You sent my maid away," she replied, "and I will require assistance in undressing."

"I am here to serve." Augustin set her down on the edge of the bed.

Eyreka could not help but notice that the hunger was gone, buried once again beneath the icy gray of his gaze. She knew he had himself back under control by the way he stood, stiffly at attention.

Greatly relieved, she nodded. "My thanks." She turned her

back to him, ignoring the nagging question hammering in the back of her mind. Why did she trust him?

He bent down and untied the belted girdle she wore. As he peeled the first layer of clothing from her, the air between them crackled with tension.

When he reached for her chainse, she stayed his hands. "I think I will sleep in this tonight." Her voice sounded breathless, and she chastised herself for not being able to resist the powerful form of her new husband. She sought his gaze, hoping to see whether or not he too was unsettled by their closeness, or if she alone suffered.

The heat in his gaze scorched her. Pinpricks of awareness heightened her reaction to him. He drew her into his embrace and paused a heartbeat before brushing his lips across hers—gently, softly, coaxing her to kiss him back.

When she leaned into him, he braced a hand to the small of her back and kissed her with a devastating intensity that awakened the passions she had buried alongside her husband—Addison—by the breath of Odin. How could she forget the love of her life? Her ardor cooled instantly, and she pushed away from Augustin.

His bewilderment was replaced by irritation. Before she could speak, an invisible wall was erected between them. His reaction unnerved her and was as if he were two men: the hot-blooded man, and the icy cold warrior.

"I leave you to your sleep." Turning on his heel, he strode to the door, anger punctuating his footsteps.

Eyreka wished she knew what he was thinking. Before he had turned away, she'd caught a glimpse of his eyes. They had been the same color as the mid-winter ice that formed on the pond near the south meadow. Unable to trust herself to speak, she nodded. When he slammed the door shut, she knew the approachable man was gone, replaced by the formidable warrior.

Alone, she lay back against the cool linens and closed her eyes. She was a mature woman with grown sons. She would not be controlled by the passion she felt for the fierce Norman knight who stalked from her chamber moments ago. A faint memory of a Viking prophecy swirled through her exhausted brain as a wisp of lavender greeted her, relaxing her as she drifted off to sleep. She dreamt of ice storms and a warrior carved of stone.

※》》》《《《

"ARE THE HERBS your lady wife placed within the rushes not to your taste?" Georges asked, daring to prod the warrior who paced angrily in front of him.

Augustin stopped abruptly, confused by his cousin's question. "Herbs?" he asked.

"Were the odor pleasing, you would not be so determined to grind them to dust beneath your big feet." Georges turned away, but not before Augustin saw him trying to hide a smile.

Raking a hand through his hair, he glared at Georges and continued pacing. His left hip ached. It was as if he had taken a steel blade through it to the bone, but it was bearable compared to the unwanted heat of unfulfilled desire. He needed to move; if he stopped he knew he would beat someone senseless. The only person readily available was Georges, and Lord knew with the way his hip felt, Georges would like as not end up besting him.

A strong hand clamped around his forearm. He paused.

"Did she bar you from her chamber?" Georges's concern marred his brow.

An ugly laugh erupted from the depths of his frustrated being. "Nay." For a moment Augustin tensed, wondering if Georges had guessed that their marriage was not all that it appeared. But then he relaxed; Augustin had not told anyone of the agreement he made with his lady wife. His men had obviously assumed that his marriage was normal, that he and his wife had consummated their union a fortnight ago.

Would that they had, he thought, he would not be prowling

the lower regions of their home, weary to the bone.

"My hip pains me."

Georges nodded his understanding, "Let me help you straighten it out."

"Lady Eyreka does not know of my weakness." He did not want to imagine her reaction, knowing that her husband had such a flaw. An enemy would take advantage of his weakness. Is she the enemy?

"Mayhap you should sleep here with the men tonight," Georges said slowly, rubbing his chin, deep in thought.

"Send word to my lady wife. I will meet her in the hall on the morrow, and we will break our fast together."

Augustin hoped that his cousin was satisfied with but half the explanation he deserved.

CHAPTER EIGHT

"I WOULD SEE the ledgers before I hear any grievances this morn." Augustin drizzled a thin line of honey on another hunk of still-warm bread, bit into it, and sighed.

Pleased by her husband's reaction to Gertie's cooking, Eyreka asked, "Is the bread is to your liking, milord?"

"Aye."

She watched him reach for his goblet and take a healthy sip of mead and smile. Good, she thought, he too must admit that no one could rival Merewood's special brew.

"And the mead?"

He nodded, then stood and reached for her hand.

Dunstan walked into the hall and approached them. She'd heard that her sons had arrived during the early morning hours and from the look on her son's face was not happy with her. Chances were good Garrick would be of the same mind. She sighed deeply, knowing it would take time for them to get used to the new lord of the keep.

"I would like to wait here while you meet with Dunstan." Eyreka hoped he would agree to her request.

"Shall I send Lady Jillian to you?" he asked.

"Nay, she will be busy with the babe. I'll be fine." She paused, staring at her hands, not wanting to ask for help, but needing to.

Augustin surprised her. He knelt before her and tipped her

chin up with his forefinger. "Is it so hard to ask my help?"

Another chip of her pride was hacked away by the look of warmth in his eyes. "If I had my sewing—"

"Sara!" he called out.

The tall, thin serving girl answered his summons almost at once.

"My lady wife desires to sew."

Sara smiled and left, promising to fetch milady's threads right away.

Augustin clasped his hands behind his back, a movement that stretched the deep green tunic taut across his broad chest. She noticed, though she tried not to, but her husband seemed to be lost in thought, focusing on his first day as lord.

He bowed, then turned to follow in Sara's wake.

"If you have need of assistance," Eyreka called out, "I am at your disposal."

Augustin smiled at her over his shoulder before disappearing from sight.

Sara and Jillian entered the hall together; each had their own armful. Sara carried Eyreka's sewing, and Jillian her infant son.

"I hope Dunstan remembers to explain his reasoning behind letting one field lie fallow while he plants another."

Jillian smiled at Eyreka, "Dunstan is the backbone of our home. While my husband would see to our defense, his brother makes certain that Merewood's people will not starve."

Eyreka felt a burst of pride flow through her at Jillian's words. Without her sons to run the holding, Augustin and his men would be floundering. A sudden thought crept through her, tainting her pride with unease...did Augustin care if they were prosperous? A dark thought crossed her mind...mayhap he would not be opposed to running it into the ground, starting afresh with Norman crofters, craftsmen, and servants.

The thought rammed into her, making her feel like she had been in training with Garrick's men battling the quintain, and had lost, unseated by a weighted bag of sand. All thoughts of his tender kisses slipped from her mind, replaced by the growing fear that she had not considered all of the possibilities.

AUGUSTIN'S GAZE SWEPT the perimeter of the room before letting it settle on the woman seated at the far end. A shaft of sunlight filtered in through the arrowslit, bathing her in its soft golden glow. Someone said something to make Eyreka smile, causing the breath to snag painfully in his chest. The memory of the way she'd responded to his kisses distracted him.

He swore softly, turning away from the white-blonde beauty who looked up at him with uncertainty clouding her eyes. She would do well not to trust him, he thought, he no longer trusted himself ... or her. He did not ask for this union, but he had given her his word not to consummate it until they were settled in at Merewood. He had best remember to maintain a polite distance until the time was right. Then he fully intended to confront her with his suspicions.

He ground his teeth in agitation. Monique would never have doubted him. She trusted him completely, depended upon him ... loved him. He felt her loss as if were just yesterday, not ten summers past. His love for his dead wife surrounded him, softening his pain. No one could ever take Monique's place. He would not let them.

"Augustin!" Georges called out above the din of many voices speaking at the same time.

He nodded his head once to indicate he had heard his vassal. The rest of his guard lined up, flanking Georges. Henri stood scowling at the number of people crowded into the hall. Jean and Jacques, identical in face and deed, mirrored the older vassal's dark countenance. Only Aimory stood apart from the rest, arms behind his back, bent slightly forward listening to Lady Eyreka's conversation. Augustin noted that when she smiled, Aimory smiled.

Insolent pup, he thought. The lad would do well to ignore the lady and pay closer attention to the ripple of unrest flowing through the hall. Though in charge, they were essentially outnumbered. One by one, the men of Merewood turned toward him, casting wary glances his way, before lowering their gazes to the floor. *Merde!* He would not coddle these people just to gain their favor. He would dispense justice as he always did; by listening to both sides, and weighing the information carefully before passing judgment.

An hour later, yet another pair of disgruntled men stood before him. Their complaint echoed those he had heard before. Grievances so small as to not truly warrant the judgment of the lord of the keep. As one man accused the other of neglecting to repair the broken fence that divided their properties, Augustin sat stiffly erect, wishing that these people would be done with their tests of his wisdom. There would be time enough for them to see that he would show favoritism to no man.

He was tired of inactivity and needed physical action. He longed to leap from the chair, putting an end to the unending grievances he was heartily weary of listening to. Augustin's hands actually ached to feel the familiar weight of his broadsword once again.

He held up a hand and waited for silence. "The two of you will work together to repair the fence, and henceforth see to its upkeep."

"But, milord—" the one man began only to be interrupted.

"How can you—" the other started to question.

"Silence!" he ground out in a hard voice.

Augustin looked to Georges, who had been trying to gain his notice. Augustin followed his cousin's gaze, resting on that of his wife's eldest son. So Garrick had finally returned, had he? From the way his wife gnawed on her bottom lip, he knew she expected trouble. His gaze swung back around to where Garrick stood. Their eyes met and held; understanding flashed between them.

Garrick would not openly challenge him—yet.

He looked to the open doorway of the hall and watched a rotund little man, flushed in the face, rush forward. "He stole one of my swine!" The man pointed a finger at a tall, broad-shouldered man.

Augustin noted that the accused was overly lean, his face and arms riddled with what he recognized as battle scars. Intrigued for the first time this day, he moved forward to the edge of his seat, searching the man's face for a clue as to why he stole, if in fact, he did.

The man stood straighter under Augustin's perusal, belatedly turning his right side away from view. But he was not fast enough, Augustin saw the man's twisted right arm ... mayhap at one time the man's sword arm. Was he a warrior no longer able to fight, pensioned off now that he was no longer capable of fighting to the full extent of his abilities?

"How do you answer the charges against you?" Augustin noticed a hush had fallen over those gathered in the hall.

The man stepped forward, looked Augustin in the eye and answered, "I took the pig."

For three heartbeats he waited for an explanation. When it was plain that the man would not oblige him, he sat back and steepled his fingers. Tapping them lightly together, he waited. Mayhap the guilty one's tongue would loosen during the wait.

Georges shifted next to him. Obviously the accused would say no more. Rather, the other man stepped forward.

"'Tis past time someone listened. One by one, my best swine have disappeared," the man whined. "Not once has justice been served."

"I only took the one," the accused answered.

Irritated by the way the overfed swinekeep droned on and on, Augustin looked away. His gaze fell upon the accused once again, but the man was looking away from him, staring at the far wall. Trying to see what captivated the other man, Augustin's gaze swept the length of the far wall, coming at last to rest on a small, fragile-looking woman ... hugely pregnant, with tears streaming down her face.

Augustin looked closely. The woman's cheekbones were prominent, and black rings circled her huge brown eyes. She suffers from lack of food, he thought. He looked back to the man, whose gaze was still riveted upon the woman. He seemed to be silently pleading with her. Augustin watched him sigh heavily and mouth the words, "I love you."

Augustin cleared his throat, loudly. Blessedly, the swinekeep took that as a sign that justice was finally about to be served. Though all eyes were on him, he swore he could feel those of Eyreka and her sons watching him closely.

The accused stood as straight as before, with his mangled arm hanging uselessly at his side. Even if the man had acres land, without grown sons to help him plow and plant it, he would surely starve. It would take the man thrice as long to do a day's work, if that. Augustin's gaze locked with the accused. Pride flashed boldly in the man's gaze, and Augustin recognized it as a warrior's pride—the very same emotion that held him erect when the bones of his hip ground together, reminding him of the many battles fought and lives lost.

"Will you see him hanged?" Georges whispered in his ear.

It would be within his rights as lord of the keep to dispense justice as he saw fit, though not the way to begin winning his people's trust.

Augustin ignored Georges and asked the accused to step forward. Whispered conversations flew about the room, as those gathered speculated at the outcome. "Are you ready to accept punishment for your crime?"

"Aye, milord," the man answered. His mouth was set in a grim line, and his eyes once more riveted on the far wall.

Augustin looked back at the crying woman and noticed that her hands were still rigid at her sides. While he watched, two small, perfectly formed boys with black curls and huge golden eyes peeked around her skirts. The roses in their cheeks and mischief in their eyes attesting to the fact that while their parents starved themselves, the children were well fed. As he would have done for Angelique had he been in the man's place.

He signaled for Georges and Garrick to come forward. Georges stepped forward, and when the younger man reached his side, Augustin bent close and asked, "Do you know this man?"

"Aye, though he is new to the keep," Garrick answered.

"Do you trust him?" Augustin asked, locking gazes with Garrick.

Garrick nodded.

Augustin stood and walked to the front of the table facing the accused. "What is your name?"

"William," the man rasped.

"Theft is a crime punishable by death. As your newly appointed lord, the king has given me leave to mete out justice as I see fit. Mayhap the loss of your good hand would remind you that I can be lenient."

The collective gasp behind him told him that his wife and her sons did not agree. Blessedly, they held their tongues for now.

William's face turned ashen, but he did not flinch. This time, he did not seek out his wife. Augustin could hear the woman's anguished sobs. Be merciful, his heart cried out. Show strength, his brain argued.

"I accept your judgment," William answered in a gruff voice. "But ask that my family not pay for my crimes, the greatest of which is my failure to provide for them."

The man's will was as strong as his own, Augustin thought approvingly. He admired William for the man's conviction to protect that which was his to his last breath.

Augustin nodded. "Lady Jillian, please show William's wife and sons suitable quarters until a situation can be found for them."

The accused audibly cleared his throat, "My thanks, milord." William looked to his wife and sons and then back to Augustin, "I am ready."

"Are you now?" Augustin asked, clasping his hands behind his back, rocking back and forth on his booted heels before pacing in front of the accused and the crowd. *Tres Bien*. You are to begin training with my household knights immediately."

William wobbled slightly, before catching himself to stand erect once more.

"You are a warrior, are you not?"

"Was, milord," William answered, "but I have lost the use of my sword arm."

"Are you so willing to die?"

"Nay, but I could not have you believe I would ever be the caliber of warrior I once was."

Augustin nodded his head, seeming to agree with the man's wisdom.

"William!" the man's wife cried out, breaking free of Lady Jillian, throwing herself into his arms. "Please don't leave me, I cannot face life without you! How will I go on? I love you—" she cried, breaking down into gut wrenching sobs.

There were loud cries for mercy, and furious whispers demanding William's death from his own men where they stood behind him.

"Silence!" Augustin roared.

The quiet that filled the hall was eerie, as all eyes turned toward him. He noted that Eyreka's face was as pale as her hair, her ice-blue eyes beseeching him to spare the man. But he had already made up his mind; justice would be served this day. Merewood Keep's lord would be obeyed.

"I would make room for an honest man among my warriors. Come, Georges will begin your training—"

"But my arm—"

Augustin stopped in his tracks, "Do you not have another?" he asked quietly.

The man's shocked look told Augustin what he knew in his heart, the man had never even thought of using his left hand. Whomever he had been vassal to was not worthy of such a knight.

"To whom did you pledge your sword?"

"Owen of Sedgeworth," William answered.

"His lands lie to the south, do they not?"

"Aye, milord."

"Why did he not pension you off on his land?"

William swallowed audibly, shame flushing his pale face. "He had no use for a crippled warrior. Nor was he willing to take over the care of my family."

Augustin's eyes flashed, dark and bleak as a thundercloud. "Garrick?"

"Aye?"

"See that William is given a plot of land and men to plow and plant it. I will send some of my own men to build them shelter."

Turning back to William and his wife, he softened his voice. "We would be pleased to have you stay in the keep until the birth of your child." He held out his hand. The young woman grasped it with surprising strength and kissed it.

"Thank you, milord. I will be forever in your debt."

Augustin shook his head, "I am merely granting what Owen of Sedgeworth should have." Augustin's gaze swept the room and noticed all eyes were still on him. "I would do the same for all those I am responsible for." *Tres Bien*, he thought, very good. They are beginning to see that I am willing to protect all that is mine ... Merewood's people are now mine.

"Milord," the swinekeep began, interrupting his thoughts.

"Enough," Augustin ground out. The man looked as if he would argue further, but finally nodded and walked away.

Augustin turned to go, but was stopped by a light touch on his forearm.

"Milord?"

Augustin braced himself and turned to look at his newest challenge ... his wife. All traces of emotion disappeared, hidden behind the mask of indifference he must adopt if he were to deal with her on a daily basis. He answered, "Aye?"

"My thanks," she offered. "I owe you a debt of gratitude for the clemency you have shown my people this day."

The softening he witnessed in her gaze as it met and held his disturbed him. "I am merely acting as lord, dispensing what I feel is just and right. Do not forget that your people are now my people as well."

Eyreka nodded in silent agreement, though a dark look shadowed her clear, blue eyes.

Augustin breathed in deeply, rotating his shoulders. His muscles were stiff from frustration and inactivity, and he felt the sudden need for physical contact, the overpowering urge to pound someone—anyone—into the dirt.

"Garrick! Have your personal guard meet me in the lower bailey."

The younger warrior's reaction was gratifying. Augustin had caught him off guard. "'Tis time your warriors tested their mettle against mine."

With a nod to his wife, Augustin quit the room, his long strides heading purposefully toward the next battle to be waged. Though the first skirmish had been won, he had the gut feeling that the second would be more of a challenge, but far more rewarding in the long run.

He would discover if the young warrior was capable of remaining as seneschal, and if he was worthy of training with his men.

He paused in the open doorway and called out, "Have your herbs and threads at the ready, wife. Your skill as a healer shall be tested before the evening meal."

CHAPTER NINE

THE RESOUNDING CLASH of blade hitting blade echoed through the lower bailey. Shouts of encouragement, both Norman and Saxon, mingled together creating an unholy din. Eyreka tried to follow her husband, only to be stopped by Aimory. "Milord wants you to rest your ankle." He frowned at the way she continued to limp toward the staircase.

"I was merely doing as my husband bid," she said, trying to hide the consternation she felt at being openly confronted by the tall young knight in her own hall.

Aimory grinned at her and reached out to lift her up in his arms. She stepped to the side, and before he could compensate for the movement, he was cuffed on the back of his head from behind by another of her husband's guard. Eyreka could not remember if he was Jean or Jacques; the brothers were identical twins, save for their temperaments.

The older knight rubbed the edge of his hand, "Your head grows harder with age, de Noir."

Aimory grinned, "Aye. Though in truth, I owe it all to you and Jean."

Jacques, Eyreka thought with a sigh. Too bad, he was the less friendly of the two. She braced herself, preparing for the verbal arrow the warrior would undoubtedly sling.

"Milord requests that you remain in the hall," he said. "I am to send your maidservant for your healing herbs." His words belied the look on his face. It obviously pained him greatly to have to address her directly.

She nodded, waiting for the dig the warrior could never resist adding. Jacques did not disappoint her, he mumbled, "Though, no Saxon woman is worthy of being called lady."

Ignoring the muttered words, she tamped down on the surge of anger that rose within her. She had to find a way to communicate with the Norman guard. Until she did, there was little hope of Garrick's men forging an alliance of any kind with the unapproachable warriors. Garrick's men were loyal to her, and until the Norman knights respected her, the Saxon guard would continue to be wary of them. Silence was the only tool she had at the moment.

"I will do as my husband requests." She watched the Norman warrior's eyes narrow to slits of dark gray. The anger in his gaze chilled her to the bone.

Aimory chose that moment to intervene. "I will wait with Lady Eyreka." He ground out the words as if he were actually challenging the older knight, then added, "Sara was headed toward the kitchen."

The two warriors stood a breath apart, jaws clenched in anger, muscles twitching in readiness for battle. Eyreka recognized the signs well, having raised three boys of her own. She knew she had to do something or else the two thick-headed men would be pounding on one another before she drew her next breath. The progress Augustin had made just moments before would be for naught.

She laid a hand on the younger man's shoulder, stopping him cold. He turned and looked at her. Jacques used the distraction to his benefit, slamming his fist into the younger man's jaw. Aimory's head snapped back with a force that had the younger knight reeling.

"Do you not remember Monique?" Jacques challenged.

The mention of another woman's name filled her with dread.

Eyreka could not stop herself from asking, "Who is Monique?"

"You are not fit to speak her name," Jacques bit out.

"But what of Angelique?" Aimory asked, "What of his plans for her?" The mention of yet another woman's name caught Jacques off guard; Aimory lost no time in placing his large hands in the middle of Jacques's chest and shoved him backward.

"Who is Angelique?" Eyreka knew instinctively something was wrong. Something dreadful had happened, or was about to happen, and it definitely concerned these two women. Who were they? Where were they? Would they be joining her husband soon? By Odin, did the man have two lemans?

Jacques turned toward her, hatred radiating from every pore in his body. "Ask your husband." He turned, without bowing to her, and walked out of the room. His blatant show of dishonor hurt, but she would survive.

Eyreka had the eerie feeling that she was being watched, but when she turned around, no one was there. The echo of booted heels hitting the planked floor was the only indication that someone had been there.

She would learn to react more quickly; it would not do to be caught unaware. Shrugging her shoulders, she pushed the disturbing thought from her mind. The main goal she would strive for would be to get along with her husband's men, even if it killed her.

"WILLIAM!" AUGUSTIN CALLED. The lean warrior bore little resemblance to the defeated-looking man who had faced him an hour before. He stood before him outfitted in a mailed shirt, slightly dented helm, and broadsword. But it was the determined look in the man's eyes that reassured Augustin he had not made an error in judgment. William was a highly skilled warrior, someone to be wary of. All he had lacked was the confidence.

He then turned and nodded to Henri, the oldest and most experienced fighter in his guard. Henri stepped forward and nodded toward William. They stood slightly hunched over, sword arms extended, blades nearly touching. Henri struck first, hitting William with the flat of his blade against his good arm. The blow seemed to startle the younger man; he tensed and waited for the next blow.

Henri rained blow after blow, each time getting closer to his goal, William's neck. But with each blow, William gripped his broadsword tighter in his left hand. When Henri moved in for the final blow, William brought his sword up with all of the strength he possessed, knocking Henri's sword right out of his hands.

A hushed silence followed while the men stood eyeing one another. Finally Augustin spoke, "Well done, William. You shall begin training with your left arm immediately." He turned and looked at his vassal, "Henri will work with you."

At this the older man nodded. Augustin continued, "When William is ready, he can begin working with the pages. There is much they could learn from him."

When Augustin turned back around, Jacques's face was blazing in anger and Patrick seemed too pleased by Jacques's reaction. Before Augustin or Garrick could prevent it, the two warriors were circling one another like rival dogs. The air surrounding them burned with the curses they flung at one another. "You have no right," Patrick challenged, lunging at the other knight.

Jacques spun around, the speed and movement adding power to the blow he intended to level Patrick with. But Patrick sidestepped the brute force of the blow and countered with a wicked arcing movement.

Their moves were blurred by the speed with which they struck out at one another. The sharp sound of steel scraping against steel continued to ring through the bailey.

Garrick moved to stop the warriors, but Augustin grabbed onto his forearm and shook his head. They watched in silence as the two men fought. "They are out for blood," Garrick sounded surprised.

"Did you think they intended to court one another?" Augustin countered.

"Nay, but Patrick knows how important the alliance is to my mother." Garrick glared at the man standing at his side. A fleeting look of surprise flashed in the man's eyes before they grew cold.

"I suspect there is more to this than either of us are aware," Augustin ground out.

Patrick spun on the balls of his feet and double-handed his sword, adding to the power of his blow. Jacques stumbled and for a split second, grim awareness filled his eyes.

"Enough!" Augustin and Garrick bellowed simultaneously as Patrick's blade sliced down and connected. The Norman warrior doubled over and fell to the ground, gripping his bloody thigh.

"Patrick!" Garrick's tone brooked no argument, the warrior straightened and walked toward the fallen man.

"Why?" Garrick asked, nodding his head at the bleeding warrior.

The look of hatred that flashed in Patrick's eyes lasted only a split second before a look of belligerence took its place. Garrick knew then that the only one who would get an answer out of the man was his vassal, MacInness. But MacInness was in the Highlands with two of his other trusted men and Garrick's youngest brother.

"You will report to Ceredig at dawn, after you have finished outfitting all of our destriers with new shoes, you will muck out the stables."

Patrick turned his head away. "Aye."

Augustin chose to remain silent during their discussion. He would not intervene between Garrick and the other man yet. He would have been more harsh with the vassal, but time would tell whether or not the menial tasks would accomplish what a beating might not.

"Georges. Henri. Carry Jacques into the hall. My wife will be waiting to tend to his injuries."

The black look that Jacques leveled at him nearly had him call the men back, but Augustin had appearances to maintain. He would speak to Jacques later. He would either get the truth out of the man, or tear a strip off his stubborn hide.

He turned to face Garrick. "Care to test your skill?"

Garrick's face lost all expression. "Now?"

Augustin nodded.

He landed the first blow, but Garrick was quick to sidestep the next one. As he spun about, Augustin tried to catch him in the back of the knees with the flat of his blade, but Garrick jumped up in the air, the bottoms of his feet brushing across the broadsword as it swished through empty air.

It was Garrick's turn to land a crushing blow. The shock of it had Augustin trying to steady himself, almost knocking him right off of his feet. He shifted his step to a wider stance and almost fell to his knees in pain as his left hip froze. He tried to cover the weakness by feinting to the right, drawing Garrick's attention there.

Garrick's eyes were narrowed in concentration; he did not seem to notice the weakness in his opponent. Augustin met him blade for blade. Garrick was a worthy adversary, fighting with the skill of a seasoned warrior. Augustin knew he would gladly have a warrior with Garrick's level of skill fighting alongside him in battle.

Augustin took a step back away from Garrick, who was doubled over, leaning his elbows on his knees to catch his breath. Taking his helm from his head, Augustin shook the sweat from his eyes.

His page stood ready with a bucket of water. As the lad poured the cool water over Augustin's head, he groaned aloud, "'Tis brutally hot today."

Garrick drew in a sharp breath as the water sluiced over his sweat-drenched body. "Aye, mayhap you'd care to join me for a swim?" he offered.

Augustin raised an eyebrow in silent question, and Garrick

laughed aloud, "Has my mother seen that look yet?"

"What look?" Augustin asked, confused.

"Never mind. The stream is just outside the walls." Garrick paused, "You can take one of your men along for protection, if you feel the need."

Augustin let the taunt slide off him, rather than acknowledge a direct hit to his ego. "You carry on like an old woman. Lead on." He waved his hand. Though he wanted to get back to check on Jacques to see how his injury fared, Augustin knew he should be in capable hands. For Jacques's sake, he hoped that Eyreka was as talented a healer as she claimed.

CHAPTER TEN

EYREKA COULD NOT stop her involuntary cry of anguish when she saw the injured warrior being half-carried into the hall.

"What happened?"

Henri pinned her with an angry glare, "Ask your son's vassal."

"Patrick?"

The man didn't reply. He stared intently at her, then down at the pale-faced warrior at his side and grunted.

Eyreka stood up and limped over to the table. "Not long on words, is he?" Digging into her basket of herbs, rummaging through her supplies, she set out what she needed on the table. "Sara!" she called out. "Bring the heated water!"

Her maidservant entered the room moments later, carrying a tray of steaming bowls. Sara laid the tray on the long oak table and started to sort through the pile of linen strips Eyreka had laid out.

"I thought you were the healer, mistress," Henri said, glancing at the maidservant.

Mentally cataloguing her most potent herbs, and counting the number of ways she could bring on stomach cramping, calmed her. It felt good knowing she could bring the arrogant warrior to his knees, but now was not the time. Mayhap later, when their two peoples had become accustomed to one another. If necessary, she could exact retribution then.

She soaked the first cloth in the hot water, wrung part of the water out, and began the arduous task of removing the outer layer of dirt and blood from Jacques's leg.

His eyes never wavered. She could all but feel his heated gaze on the top of her head as she bent to the task. It was almost as if he challenged her to make a mistake. Despite her bid to be gentle, she heard his breath catch in his throat more than once. Each time she heard the sound, she looked up to find him studying the wall six inches above her head. She almost felt sorry for him. He had to be in pain, though he'd probably die before admitting to such a weakness.

Finally, the wound was cleansed and ready for threads. "Would you like a cup of mead, before I begin to sew the wound together?"

Jacques looked at her and then down at the raw, jagged slice that arced across the top of his thigh. "Aye."

Eyreka nodded to one of the younger servants who brought him a cup. "Drink," she urged. After he emptied the cup, she talked Jacques through the worst of it while calmly and efficiently sewing him back together. They were both greatly relieved when she tied off the last thread. He tried to stand, but she placed her hands upon his shoulders and chided him, "You are not finished yet. I must wrap the wound, else you will fill it back up with dirt."

Jacques's gaze lingered on her for a moment, then he let out a loud sigh of exasperation and commanded, "Get it done."

Eyreka could barely suppress a snort of irritation. Shaking her head, she realized it was the nature of the male beast to become surly while being patched back together.

She wound the bandage around his leg, then tucked the loose end underneath the wrapped bottom edge to secure it. "Finished," she announced cheerily.

For the first time since she met the warrior, he addressed her directly. "Milady," he said in a gruff voice, "you have my gratitude."

Her eyes welled up with tears at his thanks. Mayhap the task she had set for herself was not insurmountable. She would win the Norman soldiers over, one at a time. She swallowed the emotion … no one must guess how badly she needed the alliance to work, not even her own sons.

"Be careful not to overdo," she warned. "The threads need a day or so to bind the wound together."

He nodded and bowed to her before turning around and limping out of the hall.

Henri and Georges filed out behind him, neither saying a word.

"Eyreka!" Jillian called out from the bottom of the stairs.

Something was wrong; she recognized the urgency in Jillian's voice. "What is it?"

"'Tis William's wife, Mary. She's in labor." Jillian turned around to speak to one of the serving women who was halfway down the stairs.

"Come." Eyreka limped toward her, urging her up the steps. "We may not have much time. The shock of nearly losing her husband this morning may have brought on an early laboring."

⫸⫷

EYREKA WIPED THE sweat from Mary's brow with a cool, damp cloth. "Why did you not tell us you were in labor?"

Mary grimaced in pain, struggling to breathe deeply.

"Easy, now," Jillian soothed, "just a little longer. You're doing fine."

"I was afraid of being put to bed, while my husband faced our new lord alone."

Jillian nodded her understanding, "I would have done the same."

Eyreka placed her hand on Mary's taut belly and felt the beginnings of another contraction. "Did your pains begin during the night?"

Mary nodded.

Eyreka silently calculated the hours and the strength of Mary's contractions. It was nearly time. She looked up at Jillian. "Get behind the birthing chair and brace her if she needs it. She may find it easier to push."

Mary bit down on the leather strap rather than cry out and disturb her boys sleeping in the next room.

"That's it, now, push," Eyreka ordered. "Give it all you've got. Almost there—"

The lusty cry of the newborn babe echoed through the solar. Mary lay back, exhausted, but smiling.

"Is it another boy, then?" she asked weakly.

Eyreka's voice snagged in her throat as her emotions tangled. It was a girl, envy and joy tangled together until she didn't know whether to give in to the jealousy, or the laughter.

She thought of her own daughter, Freya. Garrick's twin had been stillborn. While Garrick had been wide-eyed from the first, Freya's eyes had never opened. While her eldest had cried lustily, Freya's tiny mouth had been closed, like a tiny rosebud. She never drew a breath. The babe never had the chance to bloom and grow, but her brothers had all come wailing into the world, and as yet fought to find their rightful places in it.

She struggled to dislodge the lump of emotion from her throat to speak, "Nay, lass, 'tis a beautiful daughter." Eyreka swiftly counted fingers and toes and began the arduous job of cleaning both the babe and her mother. Tears fell unchecked, but Eyreka did not have the time to indulge in a good cry, so she wiped her eyes with the back of her sleeve and whispered a prayer of thanks to her Viking gods, and just for good measure, Addison's Christian god, for the safe delivery of the babe.

Mary's eyes were tear-filled when Eyreka handed her the tiny, swaddled bundle. Jillian smiled, then sniffed back her own tears as she rolled up the soiled linens and began to straighten the chamber.

"Eyreka!" Augustin's voice bellowed loud enough to startle the sleeping babe, who promptly wailed in protest.

Eyreka bent to soothe the babe, before turning back around to face her overloud husband.

"Mon Dieu, I did hear an infant. What goes on here?" he demanded from the doorway.

She rushed over to him, and grabbed hold of his arm in an attempt to steer him right back out of the chamber. But he would not be budged. She sighed and answered, "If you'll lower your voice, you'll see the miracle that resulted from your wisdom earlier today."

Shaking his head as if he did not understand, Augustin walked slowly into the chamber. His eyes instantly riveted on the mother gently rocking the babe in her arms. When Mary smiled, he smiled. When the babe suddenly let out a lusty wail, he frowned.

Eyreka had to smile at that. Her husband's actions actually soothed her. Deep down, he was a caring man, one affected by the sight of a newborn babe at her mother's breast. She started to speak, but he cut her off.

"William is a lucky man," he said to the new mother. "I must apologize, with all that transpired earlier today, I neglected to ask your name." Augustin appeared bothered by his oversight.

"Mary," the woman said hesitantly. "My name is Mary."

She smiled down at the tiny bundle in her arms, "And my daughter's name shall be Mercy, for without your intervention, my husband would have forfeited his life, and I would have lost our babe."

Augustin cleared his throat and looked away.

Eyreka walked to the bed and tucked Mary and Mercy in. "I want you to rest now. The babe will be rooting around for more of a taste of mother's milk soon enough."

Mary nodded tiredly and closed her eyes.

Eyreka spoke quietly to Sara and motioned for Jillian to follow her out of the room. On her way past Augustin, she grabbed hold of his arm and pulled him from the room. She wondered how long he would have stood there staring at the new mother and babe had she not roused him from his state of semi-awareness.

"'Tis a beautiful sight, isn't it?"

Augustin cleared his throat again, and nodded.

"I always wanted a daughter," Eyreka whispered, not thinking anyone would hear.

Jillian softly answered, "I, too, would love to have a daughter, someone for little Alan to learn to watch over."

Augustin smiled to himself, he seemed pleased about something. Eyreka was not sure why he smiled, but she thought it had something to do with Mercy's birth. She took a deep breath to clear her head and felt the energy drain from her body, as the day's events suddenly crashed in on her. She felt weak with fatigue, but before she could steady herself, Augustin's strong arm wrapped around her back, as he guided her into the second upper chamber.

"You have overworked yourself, wife."

"It is my job as the keep's healer to be where I am needed, when I am needed."

"What if the babe decided to come in the middle of the night?"

"The hour matters not." Eyreka's entire body started to ache. "I just need to close my eyes for a few minutes," she said sleepily.

Augustin swept his wife into his arms, grudgingly admitting that she was more skilled than he had hoped. Not only had she treated one of his men, efficiently and without complaint, but she had barely had the time to clean up after one disaster, when she was summoned to yet another.

Aye, he thought, she was a skilled healer, but could he trust her with his daughter's life? Augustin knew that until he heard the truth admitted from his wife's tempting mouth, that she did in fact plot and plan to trap him into marriage, he could not in good conscience bring his daughter to live at Merewood.

As he laid her down upon the bed, thoughts of another woman bombarded him. Eyreka's fair hair rippled across the bed linens, but he did not see what was there. He saw beyond to what his mind conjured up ... tresses black as midnight framing a petite, dark beauty, so fragile he was afraid to touch her. Fearful that in his awkwardness, he would bruise her milk-white skin; or worse still, that she would break beneath his warrior's hands.

"Monique," he whispered reverently, before bending down to brush his lips across her brow.

"Mmmmm, Addison," came the breathy reply.

The mention of her first husband's name broke through his vivid daydream of his wife, and Augustin was confronted with the very real woman who lay soft and pliant, lips pursed to receive a kiss. He knew she was not aware it was he who kissed her.

He shook his head to clear it. He had trouble separating his present wife from the one he held in his heart. His new wife was a disturbing distraction. He'd married her to please his king, and to provide a home and mother for his daughter. He brooded over their agreement to wait until they had settled in at Merewood before coming together as man and wife.

Augustin clenched his jaw against the conflicting emotions that raged through him. He did not want a wife at all, yet he had one. He did not want to desire her, yet his body ached with it. He wondered if his wife daydreamed of her first husband, too. When they finally consummated their marriage, who would she be thinking of?

Eyreka rolled onto her side and sighed. Augustin swore under his breath and stepped back away from the bed, disgusted with his lack of focus. Daydreaming of his dead wife would only lead to trouble—his. To be caught unaware while living among the Saxon people of Merewood Keep could very well be the last mistake he made on this sweet earth.

To treat their mistress poorly would not be wise either, his conscience warned. Augustin pulled the woolen cover up over his sleeping wife's shoulders. She appeared so calm and capable while awake. Yet while she slept, and all of her defenses were down, he would swear that she needed protecting.

Later, in his own bed belowstairs with the guards, Augustin slept restlessly, throwing off the linen covering as the recurring dream began to take hold. He watched as if it were happening to someone else.

The warrior paced the chamber, fury building with each step he took. His wife was in pain and he was helpless to do anything but watch.

The slender wisp of a woman, huge with child, cried out softly from the bed where she valiantly struggled to bring forth the life they had created.

Augustin tossed and turned violently, held in the cruel grip of his tortured dream.

His wife was so small, too small. The babe had been struggling to burst forth for two pain-filled days and two agonizing nights.

"Augustin." The thready sound of his name drew him back over to kneel at his wife's side.

"Aye, *ma petite*," he answered, pressing his lips to her knuckles. They were so cold. He could feel himself begin to sweat while a hot churning sensation settled in his gut. He was drenched, sick with the realization that he knew what would come next.

"If I die—"

His huge hand covered her mouth, cutting off the words that had been burning in his mind over and over while they waited for their child to be born.

"Monique, don't—"

"Promise me that you will love our babe, that you will not blame our babe ..." Her sharply in-drawn breath and Herculean grip told Augustin how much pain she was in.

"I promise."

"Milord, the babe comes!" the midwife called out as his wife's body was held in the grip of one final contraction.

"'Tis a girl. A beautiful, healthy girl."

Augustin leaned down and kissed his wife's forehead. It was

cold and clammy. She was pale. Too pale. All of the color had drained from her face. As he watched, her skin went from pale to gray. He knew then that she was lost to him. By the look of sadness in her eyes, he realized that she knew it and accepted it.

"I will love you always," she whispered, closing her eyes. Augustin's heart clenched in his breast as she drew in a breath and held it. Before his eyes, the gray cast to her flawless skin changed to a lifeless, waxen yellow.

"Monique!" he cried out, pulling her to his chest, trying in vain to ward off the specter of death that held her in its grasp.

But she was already gone. *Mon Dieu*, he had lost her!

A voice badgered at him to let her go, but he blocked it out. He would never let her go.

A strong hand clamped down on his shoulder, shaking him. He looked up and saw his devastation mirrored on the face of his second cousin, his wife's brother.

"Georges … I have lost her—"

His friend shook his head sadly, "'Tis time to let her go."

The insistent wailing of an infant broke through his heart-ache, reminding him of his promise to his dead wife. He gently laid Monique back on the bed, pausing to smooth a lock of ebony hair off her forehead. Even in death, she looked too beautiful to be flesh and blood. An angel, he thought, she looked like a sleeping angel.

Sorrow ripped through him at the thought that she did indeed sleep with the angels. His wailing daughter was placed in his arms and quieted instantly, as if comforted by his warmth.

A lone tear appeared and clung tenaciously to the curve of his dark lashes. "Your mother has gone to sleep with the angels, *ma petite*." At his soft words, the infant whimpered.

He held tightly to the new life that his wife had wanted so desperately to gift him with. "Angelique," he said softly. "I am here, and I promised your mother to love you."

Only the growing realization that he needed to fulfill that promise, coupled with the weight of the infant in his arms, kept him from succumbing to the depths of his sorrow.

His dreams were tortured, but Augustin did not waken. The dark-haired angel seemed to grow and mature before his eyes, until at last she stood before him as she had a few short weeks ago, with her ice-blue eyes flashing with pique, her unbound midnight tresses flowing in a deep velvet wave down her back.

"I will not leave London!" Angelique stamped her foot. Sparks of temper simmering in the air around them. She stood with her back straight and her pointed little chin jutted out, determined not to be cowed by anyone. She was so like the Saxon woman he married, he thought rolling over onto his side, waking.

Now wide awake, he had the gut-wrenching feeling that he needed Eyreka far more than she would ever need him.

CHAPTER ELEVEN

EYREKA WOKE WITH a start; the chamber was dark, and beyond her room, oddly quiet. A pale shaft of silvery light illuminated the far corner, setting her bowl of polished stones and crystals afire. Past midnight, she thought. Her stomach rumbled loudly, and she realized she had missed the evening meal.

"There must be some bread left, mayhap a hunk of cheese." Swinging her legs over the side of the bed, she slid off the bed and stood.

Weariness almost had her sitting back down, but her hunger was greater. The air that stirred through the upper level of the holding was warm, lightly scented with mint and rosemary, herbs she liked to sprinkle atop the rushes. With each step downward, her stiff muscles loosened, but the pain in her ankle became more pronounced.

"I should have elevated it," she grumbled aloud.

"Aye, milady," a voice answered from the shadows at the base of the stairs.

"Aimory!" Eyreka placed a hand to her racing heart.

"Why are you not abed?"

"Why are you standing guard inside the hall, instead of atop the curtain wall?" she countered, placing her hands on her hips.

The stern young warrior stood straighter. "I was chosen to guard my mistress."

She tried to step around him, but Aimory followed. She turned around and glared up at him. "Must you dog my footsteps?"

He nodded his head.

"Has my husband told you to follow me?"

The warrior shook his head. "Nay, but I would not want you to misstep in the darkness."

A warm feeling flowed through her. She had been about to chastise the warrior and demand that he go back to his post, but his words of concern felt like a balm on her over-tired body. It had been too long since either Garrick or Dunstan had voiced any concern for her well-being. Actually, since the day she wed.

With effort, she pushed her dark thoughts behind her. "I was hungry."

The young man shuddered visibly. "You did not miss much," he grunted. "The evening meal had no flavor, save for the salt it had been over-seasoned with."

"Salt?" Eyreka was confused; Gertie had mentioned earlier that herb-roasted game hen would be served, accompanied by the usual variety of cheeses and meat pies.

"Mayhap you are not used to our rich fare," she said, thinking the man had little or no sense of taste whatsoever. "I'll find something for the both of us," she offered.

The sound of booted footsteps walking across the planked floorboards interrupted whatever the knight was about to say. In one fluid movement, he drew his broadsword and shoved her behind his back.

"Halt," he commanded in a steely voice.

"Why are you not at your post?" a rough voice demanded from the darkness.

"Georges." Aimory sounded relieved as the other warrior stepped out from the shadow into a bright patch of moonlight. "I was escorting milady to the kitchens."

"Actually," Eyreka said, stepping out from behind her unwanted guard, "I was on my way to the kitchens, and Aimory refused to let me go alone."

Her husband's vassal stared at her as if she had crawled out from under a rock. Unconsciously she brushed her hair off her shoulders in an impatient gesture. When the man continued to stare at her, she started to wring her hands, agitation building inside of her.

"You have a message for me?" Aimory asked, thankfully redirecting the older knight's gaze away from her.

"Aye," he answered gruffly. "Augustin wants you to relieve Jacques on the southern section of the curtain wall."

"Why is Jacques on his feet at all?" Eyreka demanded, stepping forward so that her toes nearly touched the overly large feet that belonged to the thickheaded man before her.

Georges's sharp intake of breath and muttered oath made her flinch, but she did not back away from the angry warrior. "I gave strict instructions that Jacques not stress the injury, lest the wound reopen and my stitches not hold." By Odin, were all men this stubborn? She watched Georges's eyebrows raise in disbelief. Did no Norman woman dare to question a man, even when he was so obviously wrong?

"And Henri gave Jacques a direct order to stand watch atop the curtain wall," Georges bit out.

Eyreka could not help but notice that every line of the man's bulky frame seemed to have gone rigid. Mayhap she should not have questioned the warrior's authority. Pausing to think about it, she did have to admit had she questioned either of her son's vassals, both Patrick and MacInness would have reacted in a similar manner.

Mayhap it was best not to push the men who thought they were in charge. She shook her head. She must be far more tired than she realized. She always questioned the men in her life. More often than not, they were thinking with their feet and needed her to gently remind them that they were doing so.

Aimory stepped in front of Eyreka and held her behind him, his large hand holding her upper arm with a grip of iron while he challenged, "Shall I tell Augustin that rather than guard our new mistress, you choose to raise your hand to her in anger?"

A bleak look flashed across Georges's hardened features, he lowered his arm. An eternity seemed to pass before he quietly spoke, "I shall tell Jacques you are coming." He turned on his heel and walked away.

Eyreka shuddered; the hatred that emanated from her husband's vassal shook her to the core. It had been many years since she had looked into a man's face and recognized the man's need to do her bodily injury. She had not openly insulted Georges, she thought, merely taunted him ... flaunting his directives with a smile before continuing about her business.

She had been brushing aside men's directives since her father told her she was to be left behind while he went on a raid. Men, she grumbled to herself, always need to feel that they are in charge. She smiled, thinking of the last raid she accompanied her father on. It had brought her to Merewood and the man she had grown to love. Nearly five and twenty summers later, she was still wise enough to dismiss the lesser dictates the men around her spouted. And by doing so, she ended up newly married, well that had yet to prove itself a wise decision, but she had three grown sons of whom she was very proud.

"Are you all right?" Aimory brought her out of her reverie with his gentle touch. He had sheathed his sword and held her by both arms. The heat of Aimory's anger swept over her, sorrow following in its wake. She had thought the youngest of her husband's guard actually liked her.

"Milady?" he asked again, drawing her closer.

The look in his eyes changed abruptly, leaving Eyreka stunned as she recognized the hunger in his gaze. In the soft silvery light, his brown eyes darkened with need, while his gaze raked her from the top of her head to the tips of her bare toes. She stood dumbfounded. Absolutely amazed that the handsome young warrior would look at her, a woman twice his age, with desire in his eyes. The very idea bemused her. Her youngest son was probably older than the warrior who stood before her.

Aimory misread her amazement and assumed that she too must feel what he could not hide from her. She felt herself being pulled roughly against him. His broad chest was more heavily muscled than she credited him with, but she could not get past the idea that he was a boy. She tilted her head up to demand that he stop this foolishness and let her go, but before she could form the words, his mouth captured hers in a demanding kiss. Disbelief had her pushing against his chest with more strength than she thought to possess. She was old enough to be his mother!

"Aimory," she gasped, trying to catch her breath.

"Aye," he answered reaching for her, trying to pull her back against him.

"Nay." She took another step back. Her shock must have registered, because the young knight had the sense to rein in his emotions and now stood stiffly before her.

She did not know what to say. She had never been treated this way by any of her son's guard. The thought of any of the young men who pledged allegiance to Garrick taking her in their arms was ludicrous. She had never inspired such actions in anyone else before, she thought to herself. Then it dawned on her; you have been too busy mourning your husband to notice other men.

A sudden thought plagued her. Mayhap she should be very careful around Augustin. The Viking prophecy she had been weaned on rang in her ears ... If a woman finds love after thirty summers, 'twill burn hotter and brighter than the fires that forged Thor's great hammer.

Her eyes met Aimory's. Her lack of reaction to his caresses, compared to the way her body tingled every time Augustin was near, shook her to the core. She groaned, knowing she would definitely have to tread lightly. She had passed thirty summers nearly nine years ago and was very afraid she was in danger of caring too deeply for her husband.

"I shall escort you to the kitchens," Aimory offered, his voice cracking.

"I'm no longer hungry." How should she handle the young warrior's advances? Should she tell her husband? She shook her head. He was a proud man. Eyreka was too tired to even think about what his reaction would be.

Aimory stepped aside. She retraced her steps back to the staircase. As she slowly limped up the stairs, she smiled to herself. No doubt her husband would chastise her for encouraging the poor young warrior. After all, she was old enough to know better than to entice men half her age to lustful deeds.

Slipping back beneath the cool linen cover, she wondered just what she had done to give Aimory the impression that she would welcome his touch. Mayhap, in the morning, she should pretend not to remember the incident. She tossed and turned, trying to sort through the myriad of male emotions that she had come up against since arriving back at Merewood. Two of her sons were no longer speaking to her, still angry that she had not first consulted with them before bargaining with the king. Three of her husband's personal guard could not stand to be in the same room with her and, by Odin, the youngest of his guard practically threw himself at her!

What would Augustin think if he got wind of what happened this night and misunderstood? If he decided that she was not to be trusted alone with Aimory, her plans for a smooth transition and change in leadership at Merewood would be lost.

She could not bear the thought of coming so far only to be defeated. Desolation swept through her as she lay alone in the bed she once shared with her husband. "Addison," she whispered. A lone tear fell from the corner of her eye, touching soundlessly upon her pillow.

"De Noir!" Georges bellowed.

Aimory ran up the last few steps and took up his post at the southern corner of the stone wall that surrounded Merewood Keep. He did not need to look at the older warrior to know what the man was thinking. Georges de Montgomery radiated an anger that was almost palpable.

"Do you forget who gives orders here?"

Aimory thought it wise to keep his mouth closed.

"Dare you ignore my command?" Georges ground out, his right hand resting on hilt of his sword.

"I do not forget," Aimory answered quietly. "Nor do I forget who I swore upon my honor to protect with my life."

Acute anguish flashed in the older knight's gaze before the cold look that was so familiar replaced it.

"'Tis best that you don't," Georges replied before stalking away. "De Noir?" he called out, pausing at the top of the steps leading down into the bailey.

"Aye."

"Never forget your pledge, 'tis a sacred vow."

As the warrior strode away, Aimory was confused. How was it that de Montgomery would remind him not to forget his vow to protect their mistress, when the man obviously did not intend to honor the same vow? Everything he knew about his liege lord's cousin pointed to the fact that Georges was an honorable man, with a strong sword arm and very hard head.

As the moon sank lower in the black velvet sky, Aimory thought of soft, rose-tinged lips waiting to receive his kiss. His groan of frustration was heartfelt as the need to take his mistress in his arms again nearly overwhelmed him.

"Milord Augustin does not want her," he reasoned aloud. "He sleeps on the lower level with the men-at-arms."

Each step that he took toward the corner of the wall was an echoed reminder that Lady Eyreka had pushed him away. He was too engrossed in his own troubled thoughts to notice the lone rider crest the top of the rise and pause to look up at the walls of the keep where he patrolled.

"Women," he muttered half to himself, as he turned to stalk back along the southern wall of the holding.

The horse and rider disappeared by the time Aimory paused to look out across the top of the rise and beyond. Could one die of unrequited feelings of love? He would try again tomorrow, he decided, before continuing on his midnight sweep of the curtain wall.

⇒⇒⇒⇐⇐⇐

"THE GUARD CHANGES on the hour," the blond man reported. "And there is no time when the wall is unguarded."

Aaron the Saxon ground his teeth together. He wanted the land. He had promised his former overlord to take Merewood Keep, if anything should prevent his lord from doing so.

His liege, Owen of Sedgeworth, had been caught withholding revenues from the king, and even now sat in a cold chamber in the Tower awaiting judgment.

Aaron was resigned to the fact that Sedgeworth Keep would be taken from them. But Merewood, with a Norman as lord, might be vulnerable. Unrest was sure to follow the new Baron's arrival.

The woman, Aaron thought ... a Viking, not even half-Saxon ... was worthy of more than a Norman pig. She was almost worthy of himself.

Aye, he thought, he'd take the holding, and then the woman. His dark eyes narrowed, she would pay for her part in his overlord's imprisonment.

Chapter Twelve

Augustin growled at his squire and then turned to verbally tear a strip off of Henri's hide. "Do I understand correctly? Did my wife arise in the middle of the night and not one of my men saw fit to protect her?"

Henri opened his mouth to speak, but Augustin ruthlessly cut him off. "Did you not pledge on your honor to protect and defend my wife?"

"Aye," Henri bit out.

"And?" Augustin waited for his vassal to continue.

"I protected your wife, until the day she died," Henri ground out. "The woman you brought back here is not truly your wife."

Anger erupted within Augustin. He growled low in his throat and lunged for his oldest friend. He had him by the throat pinned to the wall in a heartbeat. "Dare you make such an accusation without knowing what you suggest?" Augustin demanded.

The softening in Henri's gaze was Augustin's undoing. "Aye, my friend, I would."

The compassion in the other man's eyes tormented him. "What makes you think I have not yet bed my wife?" Augustin asked in a low voice.

"Because you hold Monique close to your heart and would not dare to tarnish the love you had for her by bedding your Saxon bride." Henri said the word Saxon as if it left a bitter taste upon his tongue.

Augustin should not have been so surprised that his vassal, the oldest of his friends, had guessed that all was not well with his marriage, though Henri was wrong about the reasoning behind his decision. Far from it. He was plagued by his new wife. Every time he walked into a room where she happened to be, awareness sliced through him. Though he hated to admit to the weakness, he had begun to crave the sound of her low, sweet voice.

He did not want anyone else to know the state of his marriage, or the wrong person may overhear and decide to do away with Merewood Keep's newest lord.

"I trust that you have told no one of this?"

Henri's face mottled red with anger. "I do not gossip like an old woman."

"See that you do not."

Henri nodded, turned on his heel and quit the room. Augustin put his hands behind his back and walked to the other side of the room. By the third time he crossed it, he heard the sound of his wife's voice. He stopped and looked up. Eyreka's eyes were heavy with exhaustion with purplish-black smudges beneath them. Her limp was more noticeable, though she was obviously trying hard to hide the fact from him.

He strode across to her and took her arm, gently leading her to an empty seat at the table. "Sara!" he bellowed. "Bring food to break our fast."

The room fell silent for a heartbeat before servants started moving about again, creating an undercurrent of sound and movement that was not noticeable until it had ceased.

"Thank you, milord. Though mayhap next time, you need not bellow. Sara was standing close enough that you may have damaged her hearing."

Augustin paused and turned to look at his wife. The woman dared to instruct him on how to treat his servants? The idea was beyond him. Monique would never have dared to tell him what to do, or how to do it.

Before he could answer her, Jean strode into the room, his hand on the hilt of his sword. Augustin acknowledged him with the nod of his head. Jean walked over to the table, looked directly at him, completely ignoring Eyreka. Augustin could not believe that one of his men would insult his wife in such a way.

"Do you not see my wife?" he asked in a cold, clear voice.

Jean looked as if he had not heard him. Augustin leaned forward across the table, nearly crushing the crusty trencher filled with wedges of cheese and hunks of honey-drizzled bread. "Bow to my wife," Augustin bit out. The urge to plow his fist into Jean's smug face, one of his own men, was nearly overwhelming. Only the look of uncertainty in his wife's eye stopped him.

"Mayhap Jean was so intent on delivering his message, he did not notice I was here."

Augustin could not believe what he was hearing. His lady wife had just been openly insulted in front of a room filled with servants, who now stared at her, and she was suggesting that the warrior had not seen her.

"I cannot believe that you would even suggest—" he started, before she cut him off.

"I believe, husband," she said, laying a hand on his forearm, "that Jean has pressing news to report." She turned to address the warrior. "Is that not so, Jean?"

Augustin watched the warrior's Adam's apple bob up and down, as Jean strove to clear his throat to speak. "Aye," he bowed to Eyreka. "I bid you good morning," he said belatedly. His wife smiled and patted Augustin's arm. "You see, husband, he was so intent he did not see me." She turned back to the menacing warrior, who shifted from one foot to the other. "Go ahead, Jean, my husband is listening."

Augustin thought to reprimand her, but to do so in front of so many servants would only add to the slight she had just received. He shook his head, promising to speak to his errant wife later.

"What do you report?"

"Phillipe de Jeaneaux has just requested entrance to the keep.

Henri has bid him enter."

"Phillipe?" he said smiling, "I have not seen him in an age. I wonder what brings him here."

"Mayhap rumors at court that you recently wed again?" Jean suggested.

Augustin quelled the warrior's suggestion with a look. Jean acknowledged the look with a nod. "Have his horse stabled, and see to the men riding with him."

"I shall see that the bathing chamber is made ready," Eyreka said, rising. "Mayhap he will welcome the benefits of a hot bath after long days in a saddle."

Augustin nodded to his wife. Watching her limp quickly away, he remembered that he did not want her to be on her feet too long today. "Lady Eyreka?" he called out.

"Aye?" She paused, halfway across the room.

"I want you to rest today." He walked over to her and could almost feel the stiffening of her limbs, as his wife stood straighter ... taller. In that moment, he wished he had not spent so much time on the battlefield. His ability to bark out commands did not serve him any longer. He was still responsible for so many lives, as before, but now instead of knights he had trained to do battle, they were villagers concerned with their harvests, servants trying to please a lord who could not tell them what he expected from them ... as he had no idea what to do with the servants constantly hovering about him.

"I cannot rest when I am needed elsewhere," she all but hissed the words. "You have an honored guest, a friend come to visit you, and I intend to see to his comforts."

Would that he had the words to put her at ease rather than on her guard against him. Knowing his new wife, there was sure to be another difference of opinion ... and soon. He acquiesced with a nod of agreement.

"I shall send him to you," he promised, heading out of the hall to the stable in the lower bailey.

"Sara, I cannot find the lavender and mint soap I left by the stack of linens."

"Look underneath the smaller stack to the right. I set them in the small carved bowl, the one from your father."

Eyreka found the bowl and touched the smooth rim. Her father had carved this while expecting to die at the hands of his captor, she remembered. But he had not died then, she thought to herself. Nay, her father's captor had accepted her bargain, and they had wed that same day. She missed Addison and the life they built together more than ever.

"Did you say something, milady?" Sara asked, coming to stand beside her.

"Umm, yes, I found the soap." She held the bowl filled with the refreshing tang of mint and relaxing scent of lavender close and breathed deeply, hoping to clear her mind. It would not do her any good to pine over the husband who had left her behind to see to their sons' future alone.

The sound of raised voices filtered through the closed door. "They are coming." Sara nervously looked toward the door.

"You need not stay if you would rather see to your other duties." Eyreka would not reprimand Sara, knowing how uneasy the Norman warriors made her. She understood Sara's fears. The Normans had been without mercy when they put down the Uprisings in Northumbria and Mercia a few years past. It was an impression all of her people would not easily dismiss. Her husband would have to move mountains with his bare hands before Merewood's people relented and accepted him as their liege lord.

"And leave you alone with them?" Her maidservant sounded horrified.

"Send young Janeene or Mildred in to assist me," she suggested. "I shall be fine. I have done this many times in the past."

"But those were honored Saxon guests," Sara protested, "and you were not on the brink of exhaustion, with an injured ankle."

Eyreka did not have the strength to argue. She motioned for Sara to leave her. Just as Sara reached the door, it burst open and she jumped out of the way. Eyreka did not like the look of the man who stood poised on the threshold of the bathing chamber. His eyes were dark slits beneath straight, heavy, black brows. Though not overly large, or as broad as her husband, the man still towered over her. But it was not the way he looked that unnerved her, it was the way he looked at her.

"Milord de Jeaneaux," she said, realizing who he was, striving to cover her uneasiness. "Welcome."

He threw aside his traveling cloak. The young knight who followed behind him caught it.

"Mayhap you would care to undress while I summon another of my serving women," Eyreka suggested. Before she could slip past the man, he snagged her wrist in a painful grip and pulled her back into the room.

"Oh, but I do not care to undress without your help," he rasped, looking at her with what she could only describe as an oily smile. One that would come easily, smoothly, but was not at all sincere.

"Sara. Send Janeene and Mildred." Custom or not, guest or not, Eyreka did not wish to be alone with the unsettling man for one moment longer than necessary.

"Gerard!" de Jeaneaux called out while looking intently at Eyreka. His gaze started at the top of her head, but stopped at the swell of her bosom. An unholy light seemed to gleam from his beady, black eyes.

He made her skin crawl, it was the only thought that got past the revulsion she felt for the man she was about to offer to bathe. "Perhaps you would care to have Gerard assist you?" she suggested in a quiet, but firm voice.

"And miss the opportunity of having you bathe me? I think not."

"You may go, Gerard," Phillipe said, with a direct look that had the younger man stopping in his tracks before nodding his agreement.

"But—" Eyreka started to protest, only to be silenced by the quelling look leveled at her. Mayhap it would be better just to get it done. She would speak to her husband later about their guest's lack of manners.

It was awkward, but Eyreka managed to coax the odious man into the wooden tub of hot water without actually having to watch him do it. At last he was seated, with only the top half of him visible above the steaming water.

"Come closer, milady," he said, leaning over the side of the tub.

Afraid that he would stand up if she did not do as he suggested, Eyreka decided to try to placate him until one of the servants arrived.

"Wash my back."

Making a face at the man's back, Eyreka reached for a bit of soap and linen cloth. Rather than put her hands into the tub with him, she used one of the buckets of water standing beside the tub, one meant for rinsing. She made a lather on the cloth and began to scrub him.

"Milady," de Jeaneaux barked out, "my back must be clean by now, start on the other side."

"I only assist in bathing our guest's backs, milord," she informed the beast of a man. "I shall send one of my maids in to assist you further." She stood, shook the water from her hands and reached for a dry bit of cloth.

The slosh of water was her only clue that the man had moved. She was wrapped in de Jeaneaux's steely embrace before she could think to protect herself. He dragged her closer, banging her hip against the side of the tub as he stood. Eyreka gasped in pain.

When he leaned close, she turned away from him.

"I like passionate women," de Jeaneaux growled.

She drew back and squirmed, trying to free herself, cursing de Jeaneaux under her breath, "I will not submit to this pig who tries to act like a man."

She must have uttered those words louder than she planned, because de Jeaneaux stopped and pulled back from her. His face flushed red; his body taut with rage. She never saw the man move. The blow snapped her head back with such force that she fell backwards, landing on her already bruised hip.

De Jeaneaux was incensed. He grabbed a hold of her bliaut, ripping it. She clung to one of the benches feeling the bite of wood beneath her nails, knowing he wasn't going to stop. She'd pricked his pride.

His brutal hands bruised her. Desperate to protect herself, Eyreka grabbed the bucket she had been using to rinse the linen cloth and swung into his face. He threw back his head and howled as soap stung his eyes.

The door to the bathing chamber crashed open and rocked back on its hinges before sagging against the wall, as the newly splintered wood rained down upon the floor. Eyreka dared a quick glance away from her attacker and almost swallowed her tongue. Her son's vassal, Patrick, stood in the doorway poised to strike.

Patrick's green eyes were emerald-hard with rage, his sword extended out in front of him ready to defend. She had never been so glad to see anyone in her life.

"De Jeaneaux!" he bellowed.

The Norman knight froze in his tracks; Eyreka could see the anger in the man's gaze melt away, fear taking its place. Though she had hoped to be able to defend herself against the Norman pig, she realized de Jeaneaux was almost as broad as the huge Irish mercenary. She would not have held her own against him for long.

A lump of emotion snagged in her throat. She took a calming breath to try to ease the tension there. The stark realization of what de Jeaneaux intended shocked her. The man may be a pig, but he was a very, very large, strong one. And only a very sharp weapon would have stopped him from achieving his goal.

The eerie sound of two blades sharply connecting and sliding against one another made her skin crawl. They were fighting over her. One man fought for the right to defile her, while the other fought to protect her virtue. She took a step back, and then another until she was safely out of range of the bloody brawl.

Dear Odin, Thor, and Loki! What would Augustin think when he found out she had caused such a rift between her son's guard and their Norman guest? Would he believe that she was not at fault, or would he side with his friend, de Jeaneaux?

"Kelly!" she heard Patrick call out.

Her attention refocused on the men who fought over her. Patrick now had the other warrior pinned by the throat to the planked wall of the bathing chamber. De Jeaneaux's face was turning blue.

"Patrick!" She hoped he would hear her plea and let go of the man. She could not have de Jeaneaux's death on her conscience. He was an honored guest, a friend, and fellow countryman to her husband.

The warrior flinched at the sound of his name, but did not loosen his hold. Hands beginning to shake from the delayed reaction to the violence, Eyreka reached out and placed her hand on his forearm, squeezing it gently.

"Agggh!" Patrick groaned angrily. "I can't kill him?" He sounded like a little boy deprived of a special treat.

"Nay," she said softly. "For our people's sake, don't do this."

He looked over his shoulder at her, and the menacing look in his eyes softened.

"For my sake?"

He loosened his grip and let the gasping man slide to the floor. Before she could utter a word of thanks, he had de Jeaneaux's hands pinned behind the man's back and was tying them together with Eyreka's roped belt. She thought to point out that she needed it so her hem would not drag on the ground, but the look in Patrick's eyes stopped her. He still had blood in his eyes. He still wanted to kill the Norman warrior.

"Kelly!" Patrick shouted again, this time loud enough to rattle her teeth.

"Coming!" Kelly paused on the threshold. The anguish in his eyes bothered her. What was he staring at? She looked down at her gown and shock finally set in with a vengeance. Her entire body started to quake with it. She looked down at her hands, willing the trembling to stop, and noticed her fingernails were torn and her knuckles scraped raw.

She smoothed the hair back off her forehead and sighed. She must truly look as if she had been the one bathing and brawling. Eyreka bent down to pick up the overturned bucket and noticed a ragged strip of pale green fabric on the floor. Funny, she thought, it was the same color as the bliaut she had put on that morning.

"Lady Eyreka," Kelly rasped, walking toward her. He helped her to straighten before guiding her over to the far corner of the chamber, the only dry spot, and had her sit on a roughly carved stool.

She looked up at him and smiled. "My thanks."

The young warrior knelt before her and took her hands in his. He studied them, turning them over and running a fingertip next to the raw flesh on her knuckles. "He hurt you," he said simply.

Eyreka did not want to be responsible for the look of hatred she saw filling Kelly's normally placid features. She looked over her shoulder to where Patrick now stood guard next to her attacker. Kelly's hatred was mirrored on Patrick's strong features.

"Nay," she said finding her voice. "I had just fended him off when Patrick came through the door." She struggled to smile, though it pained her jaw where de Jeaneaux's fist had connected with it. "I am fine."

Kelly's features softened into lines of grim determination, "I shall report this to your husband." He bent and picked up a long strip of linen drying cloth and wrapped it around her.

Eyreka started to protest that she was not cold, and moved to shrug off the makeshift cloak and looked down. Her chainse and bliaut were torn. Where they parted, her bruised flesh was exposed for all to see. When she pulled the edges of her clothing back together, her hand was covered by a warm, strong one.

She groaned. "Do not let anyone see me like this," she begged. "Servants talk, and our people would think my husband was at fault for the attack."

"He is," Patrick bit out, stalking across the room toward them.

"No." She shook her head. "He had no way of knowing that Phillipe would attack me." She hoped she spoke the truth.

"But it is his job, and that of his warriors, to protect his wife." Patrick's words echoed in her aching head.

"Please, don't tell him about this," Eyreka begged. "His men are finally adjusting to their duties here, and you and your men seem to accept them at last. If word of what happened were to get out, I fear what the outcome will be." She paused, "Mayhap your men would misunderstand."

"It is Augustin's duty to avenge this atrocity," Patrick's voice rose in volume. Still she shook her head at him.

Kelly stood next to Patrick, agreeing with his leader.

"Please," she asked once more. "If not for the growing sense of a peaceful coexistence between our fellow Saxons and Augustin's Norman knights ... then for my sake?"

The two warriors looked at one another and then back at Eyreka. "Aye," Patrick ground out, "I'll let you tell him."

While not quite what she wanted, it was a small concession. One that she could work with. She raised her hand to his cheek in a gesture she had so often used with her own sons, "Thank you."

"Kelly," Patrick ordered. "Escort Lady Eyreka to her chamber. I have a few questions for her husband's guard."

Eyreka stepped out into the hallway, surprised to see Henri and Jean standing near the end of the passageway. Both warriors looked distinctly uneasy.

"How long have you been out here?"

Henri turned toward her, and, from the look on his face, noticed the fact that she had been attacked, but didn't answer her. Jean took a step toward her, opening his mouth to speak; but at a sharp command from Henri, he moved back and stared at his feet.

"Get her out of here," Patrick ground out, stalking toward Augustin's men.

As Kelly pulled her along the passageway and around to the back of the hall, she heard voices raised in anger.

"Will Patrick be all right?" she asked, her anxious gaze meeting his.

Kelly smiled, "Aye. No one fights as dirty as Patrick."

Eyreka stopped in her tracks, "Fights?"

Kelly snorted and pulled on her arm to move her along.

"Milady!" Sara gasped, as they stepped into the great hall. "What happened?"

Eyreka paused and tried to smooth her hair back out of her face, but it was badly tangled and still damp, and fell right back into her eyes. She shrugged and gave her attention to smoothing the wrinkles out of her damp chainse. Noticing the rend down the front, she sighed and answered, "I fell."

"Hah!" Gertie said under her breath, moving to stand next to Sara. Gertie had her hands on her hips, and Sara had her hands to her breast. Neither one looked as if they believed her. Not that she could blame them, it was a bold-faced lie. But she dare not tell the truth. Too much was at stake.

"I was out walking, and I tripped over my hem." She lifted the edge of her gown off the floor. "I was in such a rush, I forgot my girdle and my hem got caught under my feet." As she paused to catch her breath, a few more servants had gathered to listen to her tale.

"I was on the path, on the other side of the postern gate, when I tripped and fell, rending my chainse."

"How did you hurt your jaw?" Gertie asked, her eyes narrowed in disbelief.

BARGAINING WITH THE LADY OF MEREWOOD

"'Twas the log," Eyreka said. thinking quickly. "An immense log had been rolled into the path."

As if he knew she was running out of excuses, Kelly urged her toward the stairs. He leaned toward her and whispered, "You are a terrible liar, milady."

She gave him a level look and tried to brush past him into her chamber. He held out his arm to stop her. "I'll check to see that it is safe."

"Safe?"

"Aye." Kelly's voice was hushed. "We protect our own, milady. Even if your husband cannot."

After satisfying himself that her chamber was indeed safe, Kelly closed the door softly behind him, but not before letting her know that he would be right outside, standing guard.

Eyreka slipped out of her torn clothes and bathed herself as best she could with the pitcher of water and bit of soap. She scrubbed her skin until it was a bright pink, then dried off and pulled on a fresh chainse and deep green bliaut. It would have to do until she could have a hot bath brought in.

By the time she sat down to braid her hair, someone knocked on her door.

"Reka?" Jillian called through the closed door, "Are you all right?"

Eyreka opened the door, looked out at the formidable Irish guard, and pulled Jillian inside. "I'm fine."

Jillian's eyes misted over as she touched the tip of her finger to the side of Eyreka's face. "You did not fall," she said. "Who did this to you?"

Eyreka sat down on the edge of the bed and folded her hands in her lap. "I would do anything for my sons," she said simply.

"Augustin hit you?" Jillian stammered, placing a hand to her throat.

"Do you think so little of your new lord that you would accuse him?" Eyreka asked, leaping up from the bed to pace in front of Jillian. She did not want to burden her son's wife with her worry. The news that a Norman baron attacked her would definitely put an end to any cooperation either side had been willing to give.

Jillian shook her head. "Then who did?"

Eyreka realized she needed to tell someone who would understand the difficult situation she was in. "'Twill make my husband's adjustment here as lord more difficult if I tell anyone. His knights and the holding's guard are finally on more agreeable terms."

"His name," Jillian insisted calmly.

"De Jeaneaux," Eyreka whispered, "but I have made Patrick and Kelly both swear that they will not tell my husband."

Jillian nodded, a small smile curving her lips.

Eyreka saw the change in Jillian and was immediately concerned. "They would not go back on their word and tell him, would they?"

Jillian smiled broadly and shook her head, "Nay, Reka. They will not tell Augustin."

Chapter Thirteen

The look of anguish on the youngest of Augustin's guard surprised Patrick. If he did not know better, he would think the young warrior had very deep feelings for their mistress.

"Guard her door with your life," Patrick ordered.

The warrior did not hesitate, "Aye."

At that moment the door to the solar opened, and Jillian walked out shaking her head.

"Is it bad?" Aimory asked stiffly.

Jillian turned her head to look at the knight and softly replied, "Nay. She just needs to rest."

Patrick watched the man nod to her before resuming his position as guard.

Jillian pulled Patrick out of the Norman's range of hearing and whispered, "Were you there when he hurt her?"

"Just after."

"You know she will pull through. She is suffering mostly from shock and indignation," Jillian added.

"It never should have happened! Two of Augustin's guards were standing right outside of the bathing chamber when I arrived. They did not heed her calls for help. They failed her … Augustin failed in his duty to her. For that he will pay," the Irishman promised.

"She saved my life," Jillian said softly. "Were it not for her protection, I would have been beaten to death when Harald's men captured us."

"Do not forget Owen's men," Patrick warned.

"Aye, but it was Winslow and yourself who came to my aid that time." Jillian smiled up at the warrior, gratitude shining in her eyes.

"The ladies of Merewood have much in common," Patrick said softly. "Particularly their inner core of pure iron."

Lady Jillian turned to look back at the chamber door then up at him, "Did you find Garrick?"

Patrick shook his head. "He is on patrol with Augustin and a few of the men."

"Augustin left our home when he has guests?"

"Aye. Apparently de Jeaneaux insisted Augustin go about his duties while they washed away the dust of their journey."

Jillian's eyes narrowed, "As soon as my husband returns, I want you to tell him and Dunstan together." She paused as if considering, "Mayhap Dunstan will be able to hold Garrick back."

Patrick nodded. With Dunstan's aid, they should be able to hold Garrick back, though he knew the brothers would want to tear Augustin apart for failing to protect their mother.

"I've posted a guard outside the chamber," Patrick said in a low voice. "Go back inside," he ordered, "If you need anything, Kelly or Aimory will help you."

The two warriors stood at opposite ends of the short passageway, their expressions grim-faced. Their stance identical... imposing.

Jillian nodded first to Kelly and then to Aimory before slipping back inside the solar.

"THE SOUTHERN MEADOW has been allowed to lie fallow," Garrick said, as they rode past a field that had been turned but not planted.

"When will you plant?" Augustin admired the beauty of the lush, green land surrounding him.

"My brother, Dunstan, has a plan," Garrick said; "I am not the one to ask about crops or harvests."

Augustin nodded, appreciating the younger man's candor. As for himself, he probably would not have admitted that he did not understand what to plant and when to plant it.

The more he was in Garrick's company, the more respect he had for the younger warrior. Garrick treated Merewood's people like family. Not only the warriors, but the servants and their families as well. He always made time to listen to the problems brought to him, no matter how small. Mayhap he would not have to install one of his men to oversee Garrick's movements. So far, the warrior had been trustworthy. Time would tell.

Lost in thought, Augustin had not noticed Garrick had slowed the pace until he pulled back on his destrier's reins and raised his hand for silence. Augustin followed Garrick's lead, and tilted his head to one side to listen.

"This way," Garrick rasped. "Someone is in trouble."

Augustin and their men followed along behind Garrick, riding toward a more dense section of forest. Though the path was littered with small loose rocks, and the ground uneven, they forged ahead, all the while the call for help grew louder.

Garrick pulled his mount to a stop, then threw his leg over his horse, sliding from the saddle. He ran nimbly across the loose rocks and leaves. Augustin hard at his heels, and on unfamiliar ground, slipped and stumbled to a halt beside the shallow ravine.

Augustin looked down into a young boy's dirty face. It was tear streaked.

"Stephan!" Garrick cried out, kneeling next to the boy. "Where are you hurt, lad?"

Augustin bent down to get a closer look.

Stephan's eyes widened, before he nodded down at his leg, "My foot's caught."

That the boy was in pain and trying to hide it was obvious. But Augustin understood all about a young man's pride. 'Twas not so very different from a warrior's. Neither would easily accept a blow to it.

Garrick pushed leaves and bits of twigs and rock away from Stephan's leg. The way it was twisted, it had to be broken. Augustin grimaced; it was a wonder the lad had not passed out from the pain.

"You hold him steady." Garrick's voice sounded calm. "He's caught between two large stones here. I need to move them."

The look of panic the young lad flashed at Augustin had him shaking his head. "Nay," he said, nudging Garrick so that the warrior had to turn and look at him. The flash of understanding in Garrick's gaze was yet another reason to give the younger warrior time to prove himself worthy of running the holding. His ability to sum up situations quickly would help Augustin learn more about their people.

"Augustin, mayhap if you move the stones, I can brace young Stephan."

The boy nodded and relaxed. Augustin did not waste any time, not wanting the boy to suffer any longer than was necessary. He moved the stones, and Garrick lifted Stephan into his arms.

Augustin watched his wife's son with interest as they made their way back. He treated the stable lad as if he mattered. Augustin knew many an overlord who would not have bothered to stay to help one of his servants. He would like to think that he would have offered aid to the young boy, even knowing he was a servant. It had been years since Augustin had stayed in one place long enough to get to know who took care of his household. He was loath to admit that there was a chance he would have sent a servant back to aid the boy.

"Garrick!"

The sound of pounding hooves accompanied the shout. A small group of warriors crested the rise below the keep and rode down toward them.

"Patrick?"

Augustin heard the concern in Garrick's voice and spurred his horse to follow. Although Garrick's vassal had not uttered a word, the look on the man's face had Garrick tearing up the rise after him.

The feeling that something dire had happened seeped into Augustin's bones. He shortened the distance between them and rode into the bailey in time to see Garrick pass Stephan off to one of his men. "His leg is probably broken. I'll send my mother to tend him."

Before Augustin could dismount, Garrick and Patrick were running toward the hall. Augustin heard the words de Jeaneaux and Eyreka. The hair on the back of his neck stood on end, and dread filled him, roiling in his stomach. His left hip was stiff from the day's ride patrolling the vast acreage, but he ignored it, running after them.

Angry shouts filled the hall. Augustin paused on the threshold and heard his own name used as if it were a curse.

"What goes on here?" he bellowed.

The sound of his voice cut through the mayhem, and for a heartbeat all eyes turned toward him. He sized up the situation quickly. A group of servants huddled near the buttery wringing their hands, and a handful of Garrick's men looked as if they were restraining the warrior from leaving the room. Something had angered Garrick, and it involved his mother.

Shaking free of the men that held him, Garrick lunged across the room shouting, "Norman dog."

"Garrick."

Augustin turned his head, unbelievably the hard tone in Dunstan's voice stopped Garrick dead in his tracks.

"Have you seen her?" Garrick's voice broke.

Dunstan nodded, a bleak look filling his gaze.

"And yet you bid me stop?"

Augustin had had enough. "What goes on here?" he demanded striding toward where Garrick had stopped.

"Have you seen your friend de Jeaneaux?" Garrick's clear-blue eyes iced over.

"He was headed toward the bathing chamber, why?" Augustin did not understand what Phillipe would have to do with Garrick's obvious anger.

"Do you dare pretend not to know what he did?" Garrick placed both hands on Augustin's chest and shoved hard, forcing him back a step.

Augustin could feel his own temper begin to flare. He would relinquish his claim to Merewood before he let an insolent young warrior treat him thusly in front of his people. He gave as good as he got, pushing Garrick back. Before the young man could fire another accusation at him, Augustin spoke, "How could I know what he did, when I was on patrol with you?"

"By God, 'tis your responsibility to protect my mother!" Garrick shouted and leapt for Augustin's throat with outstretched hands.

The verbal blow to Augustin's honor and his pride stung, but he was no longer a young hot-blooded warrior who could be taunted into fighting. Augustin side-stepped Garrick's maneuver and looked over at Patrick, "What happened?"

Patrick glared at him and turned his head away. At that moment, Jacques limped into the hall and walked toward him. "'Tis my fault," he said, anguish filling his gaze.

"Just tell me what happened. Where is my wife?"

Jacques nodded and relayed the events. Anger flickered, though he did not interrupt until each and every detail was repeated. The flicker caught fire and his rage burned. He could picture his wife alone in the bathing chamber, not even suspecting that anyone would harm her in her own home—or that her husband's guard would not heed her cries for help. *Mon Dieu!* It was his fault.

He turned to Garrick; "I have failed in my sworn duty to protect that which is mine." Thus said, he turned to face Garrick's men, "I cannot undo what has been done, but I can promise you that from this day forward, no woman ... noble or servant ... Norman or Saxon, shall have to fear such treatment while living under my protection."

Augustin turned and strode from the room, his booted steps ringing on the planks of wood in the echoing silence. He could not understand why the men he left to guard his wife had not done their duty. At the top step Henri's earlier words filled him with dread, I protected your wife until the day she died. Eyreka was not truly his wife. How could he expect his guard to protect her as she deserved when he treated her as little more than a highly regarded stranger.

As his steps led him closer to the solar, the self-revulsion he felt began to burn a hole in his stomach. His readiness to accept Lady Eyreka's terms, and put off their joining, had let him feel that he had some modicum of control over their situation. He had been a fool to believe it so.

The look of hatred the warrior guarding the door turned on him was palpable. He dismissed the man with a look and turned toward Aimory. The anguish in the warrior's gaze made his heart stop in his breast. But was it guilt, or fear, that worried the young knight? He would see for himself.

His hand was firm as he pushed open the door to the solar. As he approached the bed where his wife lay, his breath caught in his throat.

"She's sleeping," he heard a soft voice say.

Augustin closed his eyes and drew in a fortifying breath. *Mon Dieu*—no one deserved such treatment. When he opened them again, he noticed Garrick's young wife, Jillian, standing before him. Her gaze was filled with understanding. He had not realized until that very moment how much he actually cared for the battered woman lying before him.

"Is she in much pain?" he rasped.

Jillian shook her head, "I gave her a strong sleeping draught." She paused to brush a strand of silver white hair from Eyreka's brow. "She was cruelly beaten, but Reka is strong. With sleep, she will heal."

Augustin stood next to the bed, anger surging through him. He would hear from de Jeaneaux's own lips why the man he used to call friend dared to strike Eyreka. Her jaw was bruised on one side and her lips swollen. The woolen bed covering had slipped down to her waist, and the low neckline of her sleeping gown left nothing to his imagination. The details that he had stood still listening to were brought to life in the purple marks left behind marring her milk-white skin.

His anguish quickly turned to rage at the sight. De Jeaneaux would pay for defiling his wife this way. He clenched and unclenched his fists while his breathing turned ragged. The fact that he had failed to protect his wife from one of his own countrymen left a bitter taste in his mouth.

Lady Jillian's touch on his forearm nearly shattered his control. He blinked away the moisture and ground out, "He shall pay for this."

"He already has," Jillian answered.

"Then he shall pay again." Augustin spun about on his heel and strode for the door.

GARRICK AND DUNSTAN stood shoulder to shoulder, flanked by their Irish mercenary guards. Augustin was not uneasy; in fact, their anger soothed him. They shared a common goal at last. Justice would be served, he thought looking at the despicable Norman who stood before them. The man's torn lip, bloody nose, and blackened eyes reminded him of what had occurred. His gut twisted; how could Phillipe betray him like this? *Merde*, Eyreka was his wife. A murmured phrase whispered through his tortured mind, "She's not truly your wife, Monique was."

God's eyes, what if Phillipe overheard his men talking about his relationship, or lack of one, with his wife? The thought was sobering.

"Why did you attack my wife?" he demanded. "Why did you betray my trust?" Augustin asked. "I counted you a friend."

Phillipe tried to sneer, but the motion opened the scab forming at the corner of his mouth. He grunted instead. "I know you. You would never accept a Saxon woman as wife."

Augustin's gut continued to roil and burn. He started to reign in his temper, but saw no reason to. The man before him did not deserve his consideration, or his time. He deserved to be beaten.

Augustin's fist connected with Phillipe's jaw, and the warrior dropped like a stone. Garrick grunted and Dunstan smiled.

"What will you do with him?" Garrick asked.

"Tie him up and take him to the empty shed by the back of the stable, until I have decided on a suitable punishment." He paused then added, "Post three guards outside."

Dunstan laid a hand on his brother's arm as Garrick stepped forward, inches away from Henri and Jean.

"What about these two?" Garrick bit out. "Will you have them flogged?"

"Aye," Augustin answered, his stomach icing over. A woman had come between him and his men; if he let the feelings fester, he could learn to hate her for it. But that woman was his wife, and as such deserved his protection and regard, not his disdain.

"Bring them to the lower bailey in an hour," he ordered, stalking away. He had to speak to Eyreka.

"NAY HUSBAND," EYREKA begged, sitting up straighter in bed. "You cannot! Henri is one of your oldest friends and Jean is so young—"

"Henri made a vow to protect you," he bit out, "and Jean will be thirty summers."

Eyreka wrung her hands in agitation. Her jaw throbbed and

her hands ached, but she had to make her hardheaded husband understand the ramifications. "They have made an error in judgment."

"A grievous one," he interrupted.

"To have them publicly whipped would satisfy your own need for justice, but what of my needs?"

Augustin turned toward her and took a step closer. His gaze swept from her face to her collarbone. She knew he could see each and every bruise, but she did not try to cover herself. She needed to make him understand.

"Your men would grow to hate me, blame me for their humiliation."

"They should have acted on your behalf and stopped Phillipe."

"Why would they?" she asked quietly, "'Tis obvious they think you have little regard or feelings for me."

Augustin reached out a hand toward her, fisted it, and let it drop back to his side.

"You cannot help the way you feel, Augustin," she said softly. "You did not ask to have a wife thrust upon you."

His pained expression changed to one of distrust. Still he said nothing.

"I know you do not trust me, though I have tried to give you reason to. But I think you must first hear my reasons for wanting to wed."

Eyreka's throat tightened, and she could feel tears burning behind her eyes. "I overheard my sons discussing the king's missive and knew you were to become the new Lord of Merewood." She cleared her throat and swiped at a tear. "I thought if you agreed to marry me, my sons would not have to leave our home. Our people would not have to suffer while they learned to live under Norman rule."

Augustin raked a hand through his hair and started pacing again. "You knew."

"How else could I have come up with a solution that would

BARGAINING WITH THE LADY OF MEREWOOD

benefit all?" she asked, totally exasperated with the obtuse man pacing before her.

"Best for me and my men?" he growled.

"Aye, what do you know of our crops or our livestock?" she asked. "Did you know that when given the choice, the king seeks our mead above all others?" He started to speak, but she ignored him. "Garrick knows the lay of the land and how best to defend our holding, and Dunstan knows when the ground is ready for a change in the grain planted. Do you?" she asked pointedly.

He stared at her—speechless. Good, she thought, maybe he would begin to understand that her decision had little to do with them and all to do with those that depended upon them.

"We will speak of this again," he said, walking toward the door.

She threw back the linen cover and ran toward him. At her touch, he stopped, "Will you reconsider Henri and Jean's punishment?" She could not hold back the tears.

"You truly care." He seemed stunned by the realization.

"Aye, for the good of all concerned. Your men and our people."

Augustin inclined his head and rasped, "They shall be confined in solitary, with the barest of sustenance for two days."

Eyreka didn't smile; she was already planning how to sneak food in to the two warriors.

Chapter Fourteen

A FEW DAYS after she was attacked, Eyreka finally stopped looking over her shoulder, expecting to be pounced on from behind. She would never have admitted the fact to anyone, but the attack had rattled her. She sat stiffly erect at the table, uneasy and unsure how to approach her husband's guard. She nodded to Sara to serve the nooning meal.

Though her jaw still pained her, the swelling had gone down. She knew she looked a sight; the bruising on her jaw had started to turn from a ghastly shade of purple to a truly lovely shade of green tinged with yellow. Eyreka was wise enough to know the longer she lay abed, the longer her people would carry a grudge against her husband. Eyreka could not let that happen. Though she did not hold the attack against Augustin, she knew there were those who did.

She looked over at the empty seat beside her and then over to where Garrick sat.

She wondered just how much longer her son would hold out before voluntarily speaking to her. It had been almost a fortnight since either of her sons had spoken to her. And then only to let her know that they did not approve of her means to keep their family home intact. Unwilling to explain, reasoning with them yet again, she asked. "Why are you not out on patrol with Augustin?"

"I've sent Patrick," he answered.

"Do you think that wise?"

"I've been to see the blacksmith," he interrupted, changing the subject. "Ceredig has almost finished the repairs to the armor. My men need not fear a sword will find its way through any broken rings in their mail."

Eyreka's emotions tangled. She was relieved to have at least her eldest speaking to her again. She turned away to sip at the spiced wine, uneasy with her son's avoidance of a discussion of his decision to send the hot-tempered young Irishman out on patrol with the Normans.

She would have to let it go. "I'm pleased that Ceredig has decided to work with you," she said smiling. The blacksmith had been instrumental in her leaving the holding unnoticed. If not for his timely intervention, her sons would have followed too closely behind and prevented her from seeing the king. Only the gods knew where her sons would be right now if she had not had the courage to take matters into her own hands.

Eyreka looked around the hall, pleased to see that all appeared normal. "Dunstan?"

Her younger son was speaking with one of her husband's men, but he ended the conversation and turned toward her expectantly. "Aye, Mother?"

An improvement, she thought. She had his attention. "Has the southern meadow been readied for planting?"

He nodded his head and smiled, and a low-pitched grumbling to her left caught her attention.

"Did you salt the meat intentionally?" she heard Georges ask.

Surprised, she took a bite of her own game hen and sighed. It was not salty at all. The Norman obviously had no sense of taste.

"This wine is sour enough to turn the food in my stomach," she heard another of her husband's men grumble.

She lifted her wine goblet and took a tiny sip; the wine was potent, but very smooth. Not a hint of sour. The Norman guard obviously needed to develop a taste for their Saxon fare. After the meal had ended, she rose, quickly followed by Aimory.

"'Tis my duty to guard you today, milady."

Rather than argue, Eyreka bowed her head and walked toward the kitchens. Aimory followed closely behind her and mumbled something about the food not being fit for a beast, let alone a starving warrior.

On a whim, she stopped at the end of the long table where most of the Norman guard sat and popped a piece of meat from one of the half-filled trenchers into her mouth. She started choking on the dry, overly salted bit of fowl. Without thinking, she grabbed the nearest goblet and took a huge gulp. The sour wine made her eyes tear.

When Aimory silently offered her a cup of water, she tried to thank him, but couldn't stop choking. She gave up trying and drank deeply. He was smiling at her reaction, and she wondered if there was something she had missed.

"Milady, mayhap I should describe the daily fare your husband's men have been served," Aimory said in a low voice.

She nodded, "I think a walk to the kitchen and herb gardens would be invigorating." While they walked, Aimory explained how the Norman guard had been served over-salted meat and game with day old-bread and sour wine from the very first day they arrived at Merewood.

Eyreka could feel her blood begin to boil. Outraged that one of her own people would do such a thing, she knew she couldn't ignore the proof she'd choked on.

She stalked into the kitchen ready to do battle. "How could you be so cruel as to serve my husband's men such meat?" she demanded of Gertie. The older woman backed away, but the expression on her face remained blank.

Eyreka did not want to ask, almost afraid to hear Gertie's reply, but she had to. "Did you not soak the meat first before serving, or did you add more salt?"

The woman did not answer her.

"What happened to the wine? I tasted each new barrel

opened myself. Not a one was sour!" Impatience had Eyreka running a hand through her unbound hair.

"If I may speak," Aimory offered quietly.

Eyreka nodded.

"From the first we have been served similar fare. We thought mayhap your cook had much to learn. But the constant praise your son's men heap upon the cook has made me suspicious."

"And when I tasted the food, you realized …"

"… that we were not being served the same food." Aimory finished.

Eyreka turned back toward her maidservant, Sara, who stood beside their cook. "What have you served my husband?" she demanded.

"You share a trencher, do you not?"

Eyreka could not believe the anger laced between the woman's words.

"See that you toss out all of the tainted meat you have been serving my husband's men. From now on, I will personally taste each and every trencher that you serve them."

On their way back across the bailey, Eyreka heard angry shouts being hurled from atop the curtain wall. She hurried over to the wall with Aimory close beside her.

"And I said I cannot let you in, Norman dog," Kelly shouted down at the angry warriors demanding entrance.

Eyreka could not believe what she just heard. By Odin, when had the situation between their two peoples degenerated? Had she been so occupied trying to maintain the peace, she did not notice things had not deteriorated to where they now stood…they had been that way all along?

Bits and pieces of conversations filled her head, and in each one, there had been a complaint from her people about Augustin's men, their squires, and their servants. She had thought she handled the complaints to everyone's satisfaction. To be fair, she had heard nearly an equal number of complaints from the Normans muttered beneath their breath. She had been so focused on melding their lives together that she had ignored the true state of affairs.

"Kelly!" Fear iced through her stomach. She must do something or all would have been for naught.

The young warrior turned around to face her. At her pointed look, a deep flush started up his neck, making each and every one of his freckles stand out.

"Aye, Lady Eyreka?"

"I trust that you will allow my husband's men entrance into our home without further incident, lest I have to speak to my son about your conduct."

The flash of fear in the man's eyes told her all that she needed to know. Garrick was yet unaware that anything untoward was happening. At least it was not on his orders that Kelly acted, barring the Norman guard entrance to the keep.

She turned and asked Aimory. "Does this sort of thing happen often?"

He looked up at the scowling guard and then at her. "Every time one of our guard goes out on patrol without one of your son's guard."

It was worse than she thought. After she had begged for leniency for the two Norman guards who let de Jeaneaux beat her, then snuck food to them, her husband's men still did not fully accept her. Wishing for the moon to drop pearls of moonlight into her outstretched hands would not be enough to make it so. The problem involved their two peoples. Her son's guard had yet to be persuaded to trust the Norman guard. Her grand plan to live separate lives, while she and Augustin settled into life together at Merewood, was not as inspired as she had thought. In going their separate ways, sleeping in separate chambers, she had let everyone know that she had little regard for the new lord of the keep. Her show of respect to him as lord meant little, when she had not accepted him as a man.

In her heart she admitted that she had been trying to delay the inevitable, hoping to grow accustomed to having a husband again. But that was not the whole of it, she thought. She was afraid. Afraid of the way she was drawn to the man she had wed. The man who looked at her with Addison's beautiful storm-gray eyes, the man who made her skin tingle every time he walked into the room. It was obvious from the way her husband avoided her that she was the only one suffering.

"Are you all right, milady?" Aimory sounded concerned.

"I must speak to my husband." Unease tangled together with the growing fear that she was becoming enthralled with the last man she wanted to be attracted to.

"He is trying to sort out the difficulty with the blacksmith," Aimory offered.

"Difficulty?"

"Aye, for some reason Merewood's smithy does not have time to repair any Norman armor."

Eyreka's first reaction was to chastise the young knight for speaking out against one of her people, but she remembered Garrick's comments from just a short while ago. Her son had been more than pleased with the repairs Ceredig had made to his men's armor. How was it that Ceredig had time for Merewood's Saxon populace and none for the Normans?

Aimory left her at the door to her chamber, but only after wrangling a promise from her that she would lie down and rest.

As soon as the warrior's broad back disappeared, Eyreka opened the door the rest of the way and swiftly descended the stairs in his wake, knowing the loud commotion coming from the hall held the man's full attention. She hurried. It was only a matter of time before one of her son's guard would take Aimory's place at her door. Her husband's vow to protect had not been hollow.

She slipped through the crowd of people waiting in the hall, shaking her head at those who tried to speak to her. Thankfully her people knew her well. She needed time away. With de Jeaneaux behind lock and key, she felt safe leaving the walls of the holding.

The sunlit path led her away from the walls of her home. With each step, her anxiety fell away. The trill of birds above her soothed her tired soul. The heady scent of sun-warmed pine mingled with the scent of wildflowers lining the well-worn path toward the stream. She slowed her steps and breathed deeply, inhaling the fragrance. How she missed taking solitary walks through the wood. It was just what she needed to clear her head. Mayhap now she would be able to decide upon a course of action that would bring the two groups closer together and accept one another. It would take a miracle, she snorted. Lost in her own troubled thoughts, she stayed away longer than she intended.

Chapter Fifteen

Augustin followed Garrick's suggestion and picked up his wife's trail on the path leading to the wood.

He found his wife curled up on a springy bed of moss, leaning against the stout trunk of an ancient oak, fast asleep.

What possessed her to leave the safety of the holding? How was he to ensure her safety, if she wandered away without so much as one guard?

"Is she—" Georges began.

"Will she—" Henri said at the same time, interrupting his thoughts.

Augustin heard Garrick answer the half-formed questions, "She's asleep."

Augustin bent on one knee and scooped his wife into his arms. They trembled as the delayed reaction set in. He had failed his wife once, and the thought of any harm befalling her again, though he not be at fault for it, ate at his gut. His vows to protect the woman he had wed lay like ash upon his tongue. Words had not been protection enough against the deeds of one man, but how he continued and reacted would be.

His wife's son had been vocal in his condemnation of the Norman guard, and Augustin's handling of the subsequent punishment. Garrick had been immovable. If the two guards were ever to come together to work as a single unit, it would be up to him to be the first to extend the branch of peace.

It dawned on him that the young man was just as hardheaded and immovable as he. Though it had been days since he and Garrick had tested one another's mettle in the lower bailey, Augustin said what he hoped would show his wife's son that he did value the young warrior's experience with a broadsword. "When last we trained, you fought well, Garrick," he said slowly. At Garrick's shocked look, he merely shrugged.

While he had come to admire Garrick's talent with a blade and his cool-headed decisions, he was loath to admit too much. He had no wish to appear weak, or that he groveled for attention from Merewood's seneschal in order to gain the man's trust. But the younger man deserved the recognition, belated though it may be.

Even as he thought it, his mind wandered back to the woman in his arms. 'Twas past time to speak to her. Obviously their lives at Merewood would have to change. He grudgingly accepted the fact that Garrick was capable of running the keep's defenses. He would be a fool not to utilize the man's talents. While Augustin would continue to hear grievances and expect to be kept apprised of ongoing matters, he would not wrest control of the holding from Garrick.

The king would be satisfied with Merewood's revenues. His lady wife had far more insight into the future than he had been willing to grant her.

A dark thought crossed his mind; though he be loath to admit it, his relationship with his wife seemed to have a direct effect on the difficulties that seemed to be plaguing Merewood of late.

Gathering her closer, he tugged on the destrier's reins and headed back toward the walls of Merewood. What made her seek the refuge of the forest? Why did she leave the safety of their home?

In the stable yard, he passed his wife off to Garrick while he dismounted. But as soon as his feet touched the ground, he took her back into his arms and held her against his heart. She was still a mystery to him. His lady wife was kind to his men, going so far as to protect them when they openly insulted her. She worked tirelessly as the healer, overseeing the running of the holding, and did her best to intervene when problems arose between the servants and those who had journeyed with him.

She should not overdo, he thought. She was exhausted and would make herself ill if she did not …

Augustin never finished that thought. The startling realization that he was distracted beyond reason by his wife nearly paralyzed him. He did not love her, nor did he think he could grow to love her as he did Monique, but he definitely cared about her. Deeply cared.

Striding across the bailey, he ignored the condemning looks aimed at him. They no longer bothered him, how could her people make him feel any more responsible for the attack on her than he already did?

Jillian was waiting for him in his wife's chamber. Before she could wake Eyreka by checking for injuries, he laid his wife gently on the bed and motioned Jillian away from her. "She's exhausted."

"I'll have an herbal sent up, should she waken."

Augustin could not sit and wait. He got up and started to pace. His thoughts tangled themselves around ethereal memories of his first wife and bold images of his second wife. Monique had never given him a moment's worry. She spent her days among her women contentedly sewing or weaving. Monique had been far too fragile to venture beyond the walls of their home on long walks. Augustin sighed deeply, longing filling his empty soul. It was Monique's very fragility that had initially attracted him. Ultimately, it had killed her. That, too, was partially his fault; she had been too frail to survive the birth of their daughter.

"Angelique," he moaned aloud. How could he summon his daughter here now with his holding in such upheaval? She would be biding her time in London, awaiting his summons to join him at Merewood. He had not yet had the chance to tell his new wife about her. He had planned to consummate his marriage before his daughter arrived, but their initial adjustment had taken longer than he had thought it would. *Mon Dieu*, he needed the time to explain Angelique to his wife, and the plans he had for her future. Eyreka's tutelage was key in those plans. Now it looked as if he would have to put off sending for his daughter.

"Who is Angelique?" Jillian asked, concern filling her gaze.

He had not thought he said the name aloud. Frustration filled him as he turned his back on Garrick's wife.

"Mayhap an angel?" came the soft reply from the bed.

"Reka," Jillian cried out. "You're awake," she knelt by the bed.

Augustin walked over to the bed and leaned down, taking his wife's hand in his. The lack of strength in her grasp unnerved him, it was uncharacteristic and painfully familiar. He shook his head, nay. Eyreka was strong, not weak; she would not die on him. He did not try to reason through why he needed her. Enough time had been wasted trying to wait for the people to accept him as their lord or his marriage to their mistress. He had had enough waiting. He was a man of action, he told himself, gritting his teeth. It was beyond time to act like one and tell her he was going to share her bed this night, and every night that followed. Once he had established his edict, he would tell her about his daughter.

"Augustin?" Eyreka reached up to touch his face, running the tip of her finger along the scar that slashed across the left side. Strange how dear this man was becoming to her. Why had she feared him? Mayhap she should trust her gut feeling and speak to him about changing their sleeping arrangements. It would be better for everyone involved. She had overheard more than one servant discussing where her husband spent his nights.

"Jillian, I need to speak to my husband, alone."

Jillian looked from one to the other before nodding her agreement.

"Eyreka," Augustin said, taking her hands in his.

"Augustin?"

Their gazes locked and time stood still. The feel of her husband's strong hands encircling her own sent a shaft of pleasure surging up her arms.

"Shall I leave you to rest?

She shook her head.

"I'm sleeping in our chamber tonight," he said, abruptly letting go of her hands.

"I think you should stay with me tonight," she said at the same time.

Eyreka's hands flew to her mouth, trying to stifle the gasp of shock threatening to turn into a bubble of laughter. But she was too late. Unbelievably, her husband's eyes crinkled at the corners, and for the first time since they had met, Augustin de Chauret smiled at her. She did not doubt that his smile was his most lethal weapon.

"I see that we both agree. 'Tis past time to change our arrangement." His intense gaze never left her face.

"Aye."

"My men," he began, but Eyreka put her fingers to his lips to silence him.

"There is no need to explain. I, too, have seen the effect our relationship has on your guard as well as Merewood's people. Were our living quarters not on top of one another, our privacy would have been assured," Eyreka paused then added. "Though now 'tis almost a blessing, rumors of where the lord of the keep has passed the night will be ringing through the hall and servants' quarters."

"I had not realized that so many would have an opinion. *Mon Dieu*, save us from gossiping servants—"

"… and men-at-arms," Eyreka added.

"Children often look to their parents for an example of how to behave." he said, as if carefully considering his words. "Mayhap our people will realize that they must do as we, and meld their lives together Norman to Saxon … Saxon to Norman."

He reached toward her with an unsteady hand and brushed a wisp of hair off of her forehead. Bending down, he pressed his lips to her brow and murmured, "Rest, I'll return shortly for the night."

"Augustin …"

He ran the tip of his forefinger across one eyebrow and then the other. Her eyes closed of their own accord. She felt his finger touch the bridge of her nose, slide down the length, and tap lightly on the end of it. She smiled. His touch was gentle.

"I will sleep here tonight, but will wait for you to recover before we seal our vows."

Eyreka's eyes opened in time to see his face descending toward hers. His lips brushed swiftly, firmly, across hers. The surprised look in his eyes must have mirrored her own. His gaze darkened, and his lips returned to hers in a soul-searching kiss that stole the breath from her lungs.

Unable to stop herself, she reached up and wrapped her arms about his neck. He pulled her closer, until she could feel the pounding of his heart.

He bent down once more and kissed her with a tenderness that brought tears to her eyes. "Later," he promised.

She closed her eyes, holding that promise close to her heart. Desire and duty warred within her. Her husband's stark need darkened his gaze and called out to her, beseeching her to acknowledge that her need was as great as his own.

It was past time she fulfilled the rest of her bargain and truly accept him as her husband.

Eyreka fell asleep dreaming not of the love of her life, the father of her children … she dreamed of Augustin's kiss.

Chapter Sixteen

She was still sleeping when Augustin came back. He moved quietly, not wanting to wake her. He stood next to the bed where she lay and looked down at her. Her pale hair glistened in the shaft of moonlight that shone through the arrowslit. The strands beckoned to him; they looked so soft, he could not stop himself. He reached out and filled his hands with it, bringing her hair to his nose, inhaling the subtle, distinct fragrance that he would forever associate with his wife—lavender and rain.

He spread his fingers wide and watched as the silky strands sifted through his fingers, falling back against the pillow. He turned his back on her and undressed, tossing his clothes on top of the chest by the wall. Carrying his broadsword with him, he laid it on the floor next to the bed.

Laying down, he groaned as Eyreka sighed and shifted. He braced himself as she snuggled closer. She stopped when she wedged her back up against his chest. The last thing he remembered, before drifting off to sleep, was the comforting feel of her slender back pressed against him.

Eyreka wakened to bright sunlight and the sight of her

husband's smiling face, as he stood in the doorway to their chamber.

"Where did you sleep?"

His smile sent shafts of pleasure shooting through her. "With you." He slipped out through the door and closed it behind him.

Eyreka lay back against the pillows and turned on her side. The faint scent of mint and lavender, her own soap, lingered on the empty pillow beside her. He had washed before coming to bed. She sighed wishing she'd had a chance to talk with him, but Augustin was a man of habit and would be consulting with his vassals right about now.

Eyreka had just scooted up in bed when Augustin strode back into the room. Her heart skipped a beat noticing how his broad shoulders filled the doorway, where he stood staring at her. The man was distracting and too good-looking for her peace of mind.

"You're not meeting with Georges and Henri?" He always met with his vassals before breaking his fast.

"Later," he answered.

"Have you eaten yet?" she asked, swinging her legs to the edge of the bed.

"I came to see if you felt well enough to join me in the hall."

"Aye." She slipped off the bed and stood on knees that threatened to buckle. "I only needed a day of rest to regain my strength."

Steadying her, he frowned. "Mayhap you should stay in bed."

The heat of his touch made her stomach flip. "Just give me a moment?" she asked.

"You are a stubborn woman," he ground out.

She smiled up at him. "Thank you for noticing."

He raised his eyes to the ceiling and mumbled something in what she guessed was his native tongue.

"And that would mean?" she prodded him.

"That I am plagued with stubborn women."

"Oh," she said softly. Her breath snagged in her chest, remembering the names she had overheard ... Monique and

Angelique.

"Would one of them be Monique?" she braved.

"Where did you hear that name?" he demanded roughly, as he guided her over to the bed.

She shrugged. "I overheard one of your guards talking."

Augustin's sigh sounded heartfelt. "She was my wife."

Eyreka's hand flew to her mouth. "I did not know ... but then who is Angelique?"

His face hardened, and his jaw clenched at the mention of the other woman's name. But Eyreka was not deterred. She had found out who Monique was, she would not give up until she learned who Angelique was. If need be, they would discuss her further terms of marriage right now. He may not have planned on marrying her, but he had. There would not be any other women in her husband's bed.

Augustin grasped his hands behind his back and started to pace in front of her. Finally, she could not stand it any longer. "You are making me dizzy," she protested. "Please, stop."

He stopped in front of her and sighed. "She is my daughter."

Eyreka closed her eyes. So much for thinking she had everything figured out, she chided herself.

"You have a daughter?" Eyreka said at last. "How old?"

Augustin resumed his pacing before answering, "Ten summers."

"Where is she?" Eyreka asked, rising from the bed to pace alongside of him.

"With the king's court in London. I told her I would send for her when things were settled."

"Why did you not tell me you had a daughter?"

"Why did you not tell me you had two sons?"

"Three," Eyreka said pausing to look up at him.

"I have only met two."

"Aye," she said, her voice catching, "my youngest is in Scotland with another of Garrick's vassals, Winslow MacInness."

"I think I have heard of him ... the Scots mercenary," he

paused. "What is your son's name?"

"Roderick," she said sorrowfully.

"You miss him?"

"Aye. Do you not miss your daughter?"

"More than life itself."

"Then why haven't you sent for her?" Eyreka asked pointedly.

"I was afraid she would not be made welcome."

Eyreka understood his hesitance then. She put her hand out beseechingly, "I would make room in my life for a daughter."

Augustin nodded.

She smiled and silently rejoiced, a daughter!

"Mayhap we should make certain that no one question our loyalty or devotion to one another," he said slowly.

Her gaze shot up to meet his. She understood without further explanation what he was asking. Would she be loyal to him? That he would question her integrity plagued her, "I pledged my life into your keeping," she replied. "I do not give my word unless I mean to honor it."

His breathtaking smile nearly melted her on the spot. "Nor I."

"Well, then," she said slowly, "mayhap you could hand me the dark blue bliaut ... the one draped over the chair," she said, pointing toward the far corner of the room.

Augustin picked up the garment and walked slowly toward her. "Shall I help you dress?"

She could not find her voice so she nodded, lifting her arms up over her head. Augustin slipped the overdress into place and paused to run his hands from her shoulders to her wrists.

She could not help the moan that escaped, as her husband's hands sparked the desire that had been asleep inside of her for three years. No man had touched her since her first husband had died. She had not wanted any man to ... until now.

Augustin pulled her against him, plundering her mouth with mind-numbing kisses that robbed her of the ability to stand. She sagged against him, hanging on for dear life. Still he kissed her.

His growl of desire had them both pushing away, still holding on to one another's wrists. "I think—" she began.

"Tonight," he said, his eyes dark with passion.

When he stepped back and offered his arm, Eyreka laid her hand upon it. They descended the stairs together, each lost in their own thoughts of the coming night and all that it would bring.

CHAPTER SEVENTEEN

"Is THERE A problem?" Augustin watched his wife take a bite of meat from each of the trenchers on the huge serving tray. "Are you that hungry, lady?" Concern marred his brow.

"I'm not hungry." As she sampled yet another bite from the third tray, Augustin stayed her hand and growled low in his throat, "Is there a reason for your unusual appetite?"

His face was darkening with what she could see was anger. Fascinated by the change, she paused to watch the play of muscles across his jaw. They alternately clenched, then relaxed.

"Nay."

He waved the next tray away and pulled her away from the table, across the hall and out of the side door.

"Gertie added extra salt to the meat and bread she served to your men."

Though the opposite of what she expected, her words eased the taut line of his jaw.

"Go on," he urged.

"She served them sour wine too." Eyreka qualified, "She only tried to help. She noticed your indifferent attitude and assumed that I had been forced to wed you."

"Why did you not tell me of this difficulty?" he asked.

"That is not the whole of it," Eyreka said sadly. "There is more."

"Tell me," he demanded.

"I do not want you to take your anger out on my people, they truly mean no harm, 'tis just that—"

"They assume that because we do not share a chamber together as man and wife, we cannot abide one another." Her husband's tone softened; at least he was no longer angry. "Is that it?"

Eyreka nodded. "I heard about the patrols," she said.

Augustin clenched his jaw and bit out, "I intend to have the offenders flogged."

"But you won't because you also wish for peace among our people," Eyreka finished for him.

"We need to settle the unrest. I know you wished for more time to become used to our marriage, but I think we have just run out."

Eyreka brushed the side of his cheek with her fingertips, "I understand and appreciate your concern. But you should realize, I am almost forty summers," she said slowly. "My body is riddled with the scars from carrying and birthing my children."

At his narrowed gaze she added, "I no longer have the type of figure that would attract a man."

He let go of her and stepped back, holding her at arm's length. "When I look at you, I see a woman who is aware of who she is and what she has accomplished in life. I have survived a great many battles," he paused, "nearly losing my life at the Battle of Hastings, and I have the scars to prove it."

Her eyes widened, but she said nothing.

He fell silent. Taking her hands in his, he lifted her right hand and pressed his lips to the back of it. Then he repeated the caress with her other hand. "Monique was beautiful, but too fragile to survive the rigors of childbirth."

She watched pain slide across his finely chiseled features, settling them into a look of acceptance.

"I will be five and thirty come winter," he said haltingly, watching her face closely. When she remained silent, he continued, "I have come to appreciate that there is no beauty more pure than that of a woman who has embraced life and lived it fully."

Stunned by his words and the depth of feeling behind them, Eyreka bit her trembling lip, holding back her tears. She could hear the catch in her voice, "Then, you do not mind that you have not married a young maid?" she asked.

"I did not wish to remarry," Augustin confided. "I understand why you sought to bargain with the king. I was unsure of your loyalties at first, and not willing to trust," he said haltingly. "After all you have done for my men and tried to do to smooth our way here, I realize that I am the one who should be seeking your trust."

Eyreka was so surprised by his words that she could not speak.

"I would rather have a woman of your experience, unafraid of life, by my side, than a young maid," he said, striving for a lighter tone. "I do not have the time or inclination to instruct a bride in my likes and dislikes."

Eyreka felt the urge to laugh out loud at the idea, but wisely suppressed the urge. "I am afraid that I would not be inclined to listen to your instruction, husband."

Augustin took a step closer. "Why is it that I am not surprised?"

"Mayhap because you are old enough to understand that strong women tend to have their way in most things."

She watched his nostrils flare out and his eyes turn dark gray and knew she was playing with fire, but she could not wait to fan the flames.

He captured her lips, commanding her to respond in kind. The desperate longing to be caressed by his strong hands, and held against his hard body, overwhelmed her. She could not think, only react. His lips sped across her cheekbone and down her throat. When he could not push her bliaut down far enough to reach her aching breasts, he swept her into his arms and strode along the path through the herb gardens, stopping only when he reached the far corner and the protection of the tall yew bushes.

He set her down long enough to remove her bliaut and spread it on the grass beneath the flowering pear tree. The faint scent filled the soft night air, surrounding them with the sweet, fragile fragrance. Hidden from prying eyes, he wooed his wife until she melted into his embrace.

He laid her down upon the soft fabric and leaned back to remove his tunic. She watched as he folded it, surprised when he placed it beneath her head. "I would not be able to rouse such passion in a young maid," Augustin said, pulling her chainse over her head. "She would be afraid of my touch, unaware of the delights I could show her."

Eyreka could not breathe—his lips were so hot, they seared the tender skin of her breast. She moaned aloud as he nipped and suckled both breasts. "I need—"

Augustin made the breath snag in her chest as he ran callused hands up and down her sides, stopping to knead her hips until she moaned.

He settled himself between her legs, raised himself up on his arms, and paused. "Ask me," he commanded through gritted teeth.

Without further words, Eyreka understood what he wanted. "I want—" She never finished speaking, because her husband drove into her with one powerful stroke. Her throat went dry, and her eyes rolled back in her head. "By Odin!" she cried out.

"God's blood!"

Eyreka grabbed his muscled buttocks with both hands and lifted her hips to meet his measured thrusts. Again and again, she met him thrust for thrust, until at last she felt her inner muscles clench and the wonder of her release flow through her like honeyed mead.

Agustin's entire body tensed before he thrust into her one last time. He poured his seed into her welcoming warmth before collapsing on top of her.

Eyreka was so tired, her arms and legs did not have any strength left to move. As the wonder of their lovemaking dissipated, and Augustin remained silent, a gnawing fear settled in. Would this be all Augustin was willing to give, the sealing of their vows? Would he want to hold her in the night and take the time to learn her secret places as Addison had? She tried to swallow past the lump that formed in her throat. Did she want him to? When he remained silent, she tried to push him away, but Augustin's grip tightened.

He pulled her closer and inhaled her woman's scent. *Mon Dieu*, what had just happened? He had taken other women after his wife died. She was not the first. God's blood, he had not been able to wait to walk back through the hall and up to their chamber. He had to have her. But why did she draw out every drop of energy he had, filling in the void Monique's death left behind with contentment? Was this one moment all that she wanted? To seal their vows with the pretense of living together. Would she ask him to sleep on the floor of their chamber? One final question speared through him: Did he want more from her?

Augustin reluctantly rolled off of her, confused, and started pulling his clothing back on. He felt awkward now that he was dressed, and did not like the feeling one bit.

Eyreka pulled her chainse and bliaut over her head and brushed bits of leaves and grass off of her. She glanced up at her husband through her lashes and wondered what he was thinking. He felt so stiff now, so awkward, when moments before they had been tangled together in the sweet-scented grass. 'Twas almost as if in removing their layers of clothing, their inner selves were revealed as well. They were no longer two people from different ways of life with different beliefs. They were two lonely people, trying to lose themselves in the fires of passion. Trying to become what she now knew they could never truly be—the loved one each of them had lost.

Neither said another word as they walked around the perimeter of the garden and back around to the front of their holding.

BARGAINING WITH THE LADY OF MEREWOOD

The distance between them stretched wide. Eyreka wondered if she would ever be able to cross the void, or if she wanted to. Caring for someone was safe—no deep emotions were involved. Loving Addison, then losing him, ripped the heart from her breast and sucked the life from her soul until she was no longer a person, but a mere shell of what she had been. Her body shuddered, remembering the pain. She could not live through it again...she would not love again.

At the door to their chamber, Augustin bowed to Eyreka before turning on his heel and walking away.

"Can he not stand to be in the same room with me?" Eyreka sank onto the low stool and rested her head on the table. Confusion filled her until she did not quite know what to think. She had never thought to taste mind-numbing passion again, honestly believing that only her first husband would be able to take her there, and only because she loved him.

"Is there nothing special, then, that links two people together? Would I feel the same, had I let a stranger take what I willingly gave to Augustin?"

She thought long and hard about her reaction to Augustin then shook her head. Aimory's embrace had been unwanted and unmoving. Then a dark memory engulfed her. De Jeaneaux's face, distorted with anger flashed before her, his fingers biting again into her flesh, as he held her down on the floor.

Eyreka shuddered at the memory. Patrick had saved her from being raped, for which she was eternally grateful. Though she would rather erase the incident completely, she was wise enough to retain tiny piece. It had helped her to realize that she was not willing to let just any man touch her intimately. Only Augustin.

Not just any man would do. Yes, she was passionate; Addison had oft told her how much he enjoyed their love play. But she did not feel the ache of awareness in any other man's presence the way she did when Augustin walked into the room. Mayhap it was more than missed passion that flowed through her whenever she was near him.

More tired than she had been in ages, she lay down upon the bed, alone. She curled herself into a ball and fell into an exhausted sleep, unaware that her husband returned to their chamber to lie down beside her, pulling her close while she slept.

Chapter Eighteen

Eyreka woke to the crash of thunder. She could feel the echoing rumble shaking the foundations of the keep. The summer storm unleashed its fury, sending torrents of rain to accompany the impressive flash of lightening and resounding crash of thunder.

Once her heart settled back down, she sat up, noticing with a sinking feeling that she was alone. It could not be much before dawn, the hall below her was still quiet.

Getting out of bed, she reached high over her head and stretched. Taking a deep breath, she inhaled the welcome scent of rain-drenched herbs and grass that drifted in through the arrowslit. She walked over to it and rose up on her toes to look out over the gardens, thinking of her husband and all that they had shared last night. She closed her eyes and savored the memory, not knowing when, or if, she would ever be granted another taste.

She dressed quickly and went downstairs through the hall and out the side door, running to the kitchens. By the time she had covered the short distance, she was soaked to the skin, but the heat from the cooking fires quickly warmed her.

"Are the trenchers ready for tasting?" Eyreka asked, trying to maintain a stern expression on her face.

Gertie gave her a hard look and turned her back on her.

Eyreka allowed the insolent behavior, knowing that her cook's heart was in the right place, though her actions be skewed.

"No need to fill yourself up again, you must still be stuffed from all the food you tasted last evening," Sara said grumpily, ladling honey over thick slices of bread, not looking up when she spoke.

"I shall take you at your word," Eyreka said quietly. "See that all of the warriors who guard our holding are well fed."

Sara nodded her agreement, and followed Eyreka back to the hall to begin serving their meal.

Georges was standing in the doorway with his back to her when she approached. "I have not seen Augustin," he was saying to the men, "nor did he spend the night below with the men."

Eyreka strove to hide her smile, slipping past the warrior into the hall; she did not intend to enlighten the men as to where her husband slept.

"Good morning," she said, nodding to Georges and the handful of men standing beside him.

They paused in their conversation, and the warrior stared at her before nodding. Surprisingly, they waited for her to sit before seating themselves. She tried to hide the small smile that threatened to give away the fact that she was delighted to see such a change in their habit. A few weeks ago, the stubborn Norman guard would have ignored her totally, sitting whenever they chose. One small bit at a time, she reminded herself, she would see that the warriors accept her one small step at a time.

"Where is my husband this morn, Aimory?" she asked the tall blonde knight striding purposefully into the hall.

He stopped and redirected his steps, coming to a halt in front of her. He bowed low.

"He and a small company of men have ridden out on patrol," he said. The warrior's eyes turned from cool, clear-blue to slits of cold, hard sapphire before she could draw another breath. Something was wrong. The change in the young warrior unnerved her.

"But he usually leaves that duty for Patrick and Henri," she said slowly, a feeling of dread filling her.

Aimory's gaze softened at the obvious worry in her tone. "He shall return shortly; they rode out well before dawn."

"Then they shall need warm food and a goblet of our special mead," she said determinedly. Eyreka rose up and headed back out toward the kitchen. Before she could step outside, a large hand on her shoulder stopped her.

"I'll send word to the kitchens," Jacques said gruffly. "No need for you to get soaked again." To her utter shock, he grinned. "You're already wet enough, Augustin would have my head if you were to fall ill while under our protection."

The knight's words felt like a healing balm smoothed over her tensed shoulders; at least two of her husband's men no longer hated her. She nodded and returned to her seat.

Silent through most of the meal, she heard snippets of conversation from the loud warriors' voices. In between surprised praise for the food came the references to campfires in the southern meadow. But who would be lighting fires in the southern meadow? None of their people would want to disturb the young plants. Merewood's crops were vitally important to the survival of all of its people.

The patrol had not returned by the time she rose from the table, so she went in search of Jillian. She found her above stairs trying to soothe her squalling babe. "Is something amiss?" she asked, concerned for her grandson.

"Nay, I fear another tooth is trying to poke through his poor swollen gums," Jillian said over Alan's loud cries.

"Here, let me walk him," she said, taking the infant from Jillian's arms. "You need to eat." Eyreka turned her back on the younger woman, knowing that she would understand that Eyreka meant to have her way. After a few moments, she heard Jillian leave.

"You shouldn't give your mother such a hard time," Eyreka said, drying the babe's tears and kissing his chubby cheeks. "She has more than enough to do caring for my son."

Eyreka walked over to the table and picked up the linen cloth draped over the side of a small wooden bowl and smiled. Her son had obviously not convinced his young wife to try anything stronger than herb-laced water on the babe's gums. She sighed loudly, grabbed the bit of cloth and started to rub it gently on the tiny red bump next to Alan's tooth. He continued to cry, and she realized not much had changed since her own sons had cut their teeth.

AUGUSTIN FOUND HER pacing the small chamber trying to soothe the angry infant. Thoughts of his own daughter had him crossing the room, without a word, and taking the child from his startled wife.

"I did not hear you," she chided him.

"It would not have been possible above Alan's lusty cries."

Her eyes softened at his use of the babe's name. Her obvious love for the child shone from her ice-blue eyes. It was a familiar look.

"'Tis his second tooth," she said simply, trying to take Alan back from him.

Augustin handed the babe back to her and strode to the table. He poured water from the pitcher into an empty bowl and used the soft bit of mint and lavender soap to wash his hands. He could feel the intensity of her gaze warm his back.

He walked back over to her and took the now screaming child back. For a moment, he stared down, noticing the smallness of the babe. It rocked him clear to his soul; his own arms seemed massive in comparison, as they had the first time he had held Angelique.

He shook his head to clear out the memory that would no doubt lead to thoughts of Monique. "Have Sara or one of the other serving women send up a flagon of mead," he ordered without looking up.

The small gasp from his wife had him turning his back on her, it would not do to let her see his smile. The woman had difficulty taking direct orders, he thought as she swept from the room.

She returned carrying a pitcher. He nodded toward the table. Once she had placed it down, he shifted Alan to rest up against his shoulder, careful not to let him bump his head, and bent down to dip the remaining linen square into the fragrant brew.

Then he began to rub the babe's gums with the flavored cloth. When the baby started to quiet, he was relieved. He had thought that mayhap the child would not be as receptive to the strong taste of mead as his daughter had been.

Eyreka's hand upon his arm startled him. "My sons always preferred my husband's finger to a bit of linen."

She dipped his forefinger into the mead and guided it into the babe's now open mouth. The cries abruptly ceased as Alan chewed contentedly on Augustin's rough fingertip while watching him through tear-filled eyes.

"His jaws are as strong as his cries."

"You like children," she said quietly.

"Aye."

He gazed down at the solemn woman at his side. How could he possibly explain what he held so deeply buried within him? He could not begin to guess where her thoughts had strayed to, but he wanted to say something to make her look back up at him. Finally, he knew what to say. "I would make room for sons," he said without wondering where the thought came from.

Her head shot up, and he watched tears fill her expressive eyes. She didn't speak, but she inclined her head before turning away.

He heard her sniff loudly before she turned back toward him, eyes bright with unshed tears. "And I would gladly welcome your daughter and begin instructing her in the running of our holding.

"Is there aught amiss that you patrol in the middle of a thunderstorm?"

Augustin was taken aback for a moment, wondering if one of his men had spoken out of turn, before he reasoned that his wife knew more about what went on within the walls of their holding than he did. There would be no point in trying to shield her. She'd find out what she wanted to know elsewhere. A tiny voice, from deep inside him, whispered that he wanted to share his worries with her, needed someone to confide in, someone who would understand.

"You know that de Jeaneaux has escaped?" He watched closely for a reaction.

She took the sleeping babe from his arms, wiping the tiny line of drool from Alan's round cheek with a light, deft touch, and put him to bed.

"I had heard that you were planning to speak with him about ..." Her voice trailed off, and he watched every drop of color fade from her face.

He took her small white hands in his and held them. He wanted to reassure her that no man would ever harm her again, but Augustin was not one to make promises that he was powerless to honor. Yet he wanted to do something to ease the look of fear that flashed across her face before she hid it from him.

"Aye. Once Patrick had finished getting his point across—"

His wife smiled at his inference that her son's vassal had actually been talking, when Augustin knew she had heard Patrick had beat the man senseless. She was a strong woman, he thought, who had raised strong sons, and understood the ways of men.

"Did anyone else speak to de Jeaneaux?" she asked.

The sharp bark of laughter that shot out of him was totally unexpected. She had the wit to match his cousin, Georges. "No one else laid a hand on him," he said quietly knowing that was what she had meant all along.

She looked up at him then, "I did not encourage de Jeaneaux's attentions." Sorrow filled her beautiful eyes.

He squeezed her hands. "I know." His hands started to tremble, her nearness seemed to be affecting him still. He wanted to ask how she felt this morning, if she had slept well, if she dreamt of him, but he could not utter the words poised upon his tongue. The thought of needing to hear her say that she dreamed of him was a blow to his pride.

He should be able to control his feelings for his wife. He had not let thoughts of Monique disrupt his thoughts, as Eyreka did. Could he open his heart to her? Was it wise?

"Patrick and Jacques were guarding Phillipe." Anger filled him at the thought of his one-time friend abusing his wife. "Lightning struck a tree across the bailey from where he was being held. Both men left him unguarded to douse the fire, before it had a chance to ignite the back of the stable."

"You were searching for him this morning?" Eyreka was stunned, considering the implications of de Jeaneaux being free and what fate awaited the two warriors responsible.

"Aye."

"You'll not reprimand Patrick or Jacques, will you?" Her eyes gave away the fact that she thought he might.

Augustin almost admitted that he had knocked the both of them to the ground before he had been able to control his temper. He didn't want to discuss the reasons why he had reacted that way with her, because she was the reason.

"Nay, I'll not," he said simply. Let her assume that the men had earned their bruises on the training field.

"Augustin, about last night—" she began, before he cut her off. The tone of her voice and the way she would not look at him told him all that he needed to know.

"Now is not the time to discuss it," he bit out, angry with himself that he even worried what she was thinking.

He strode from the room without looking back. If he had, he would have seen the yearning that filled her eyes. Instead all he saw was what his mind focused on, the empty hut where her attacker had been held, and the remains of more than one campfire in the heavily wooded forest near the southern border of their land.

Frustration filled him, but he pushed the feeling aside. He would find out who camped on their land, and deal with them. Then he would find de Jeaneaux and make him pay.

Chapter Nineteen

A SHOUT FROM atop the curtain wall had Eyreka running down the steps, glad that her ankle no longer pained her. She held her breath. Augustin's daughter had been expected for more than a fortnight now. Truth be told, her husband had not seemed overly worried, but she had been on the verge of sending a group of Garrick's men out to find Angelique, had she not shown up today.

"Armand!" came the relieved cry from Jean who gave the signal for the heavy gate to be swung open. "Find Augustin, she's here!"

Eyreka's days had been filled with activity. From the day-to-day running of their holding, the distilling of healing herbs, and the inevitable small crises that still seemed to arise between Augustin's men and Garrick's guard, through it all she worried over the delay. She smoothed her skirts and pushed her hair back over her shoulders. The first impression was the most important, and she wanted to appear calm. And by the gods, she wanted Angelique to like her.

Her new daughter was finally here, and she felt as if the sun had finally come out after weeks of rain. She had bolts of cloth spread out in the solar waiting for Angelique's inspection. Whichever color the little girl chose, Eyreka was prepared to sew a new chainse and bliaut for her tonight while the little one slept.

Then she would cut thin strips into ribbons to braid into Angelique's hair.

Eyreka could barely contain the excitement that had been building inside her, waiting for the little girl to arrive. She had so many plans. Augustin had mentioned that he would soon begin the difficult task of selecting the man who would be her husband. When she had prodded him to tell her when he would decide, he shrugged and said he did not know.

Not one to look down upon her good fortune, Eyreka planned to begin the young one's tutelage at once. There were so many aspects of running a household that must be taught, she scarce knew where to begin.

"Papa!" a young voice cried out, interrupting her thoughts.

"*Ma petite!*" Augustin answered gruffly, swinging his daughter in his arms and wrapping her in his embrace. "Where have you been?" he demanded, trying to sound stern.

Angelique looked up at him and batted impossibly long dark eyelashes, "I had many things to pack, papa," she answered, kissing him on both cheeks.

"Come." He set her down gently. Taking her arm, he turned her toward Eyreka, "There is someone who wants to meet you."

Eyreka stepped forward and knelt before the young girl. "Welcome to Merewood Keep, Angelique," she said soothingly, "I hope you will be happy here."

A dark look flashed across the girl's pretty features, "I can never be happy here," she snipped out. "I will not be happy here."

Eyreka watched in confusion as Angelique turned away, swinging her long dusty braid of hair back over her shoulder straight into Eyreka's left eye. The pain was instantaneous as the grains of dirt scratched deeply. Eyreka covered her eye with her hand and shakily stood back up.

"Then I can only hope that you will change your mind, little one." Though the emotion bubbling within her could never be construed as kindness, Eyreka strove to find the emotion. The child was obviously overtired from the long journey and Eyreka tried to excuse her behavior. Being thrust into a new situation, at her tender age, was no doubt behind the petulant attitude. Eyreka started to feel sorry for her. "There is much here to be enjoyed."

"I like living in London," the young girl challenged, narrowing her eyes and jutting her pointed little chin up at her in defiance.

Eyreka recognized the display of bravado and silently applauded the child for not letting her new situation reduce her to a bout of tears.

"Come," she said quietly, offering a hand toward Angelique. The determined child slapped it away, and before Eyreka had time to react and rethink her approach, the child kicked her. Eyreka thought the bone of her shin may have cracked with the force of the unexpected blow, as pain streaked across the front of her leg.

"Enough!" Augustin bellowed, taking a hold of his daughter's elbow. "You are to apologize to my wife immediately."

Tears welled up in the cold blue eyes that stared up at her; Eyreka's heart sank. The child's reaction to her should not have been a shock. Angelique was treating Eyreka much the same way she wanted to treat the Normans who now held the title to her family's holding. But she was an adult and knew the value of extending a hand in peace rather than extending one in violence.

She was disappointed that there would be no cuddling with her new daughter beside the fire tonight. No stories of her Viking gods to lull the little one to sleep. But she was realistic, the child needed time to adjust to her new family and life at Merewood Keep. It would be far different from the one she knew at court.

Eyreka straightened up and nodded to her husband. "I will leave you to show Angelique where she will sleep, husband," she said, trying in vain not to let her frustration show. "I must speak to Gertie about our meal."

Augustin nodded, gentling his hold on his daughter. "We shall speak of this again," he warned.

Eyreka limped away, her head held high. For the first time in a long while, she had let her emotions guide her actions. She would not make that mistake again. Whether she was wanted or not, she was prepared to be a mother to Angelique.

Brushing the tears from her injured eye, she wondered what else the child planned. Making her way to the kitchens, she realized that she admired Angelique's spirit. Her anger faded slightly. Putting herself in her new stepdaughter's place, Eyreka knew that she, too, would be feeling out of sorts and difficult. Hah, there was no denying it, she still felt out of sorts with the changes at her home and, according to her own sons, she was difficult.

The evening meal went smoothly, thanks to the two maid-servants who accompanied Angelique on her journey. While Eyreka watched disapprovingly, the child ordered the two young woman around until Eyreka feared they would drop from exhaustion.

"Nadienne," Eyreka called out in an even tone, just as the young woman was about to go back to the kitchens to ask someone named Simone to create yet another special request for the little tyrant who sat on the other side of Augustin.

"*Oui?*" The young woman walked toward her and waited respectfully for her to speak.

"That will be all for tonight," Eyreka intervened before things became out of control. "You and Bernadette must be exhausted from the journey." The gratitude that shone from the young woman's face made her feel better. She had not wanted to interfere but Augustin had not spoken up. Truth be told, she was not certain he was even paying any attention to his daughter at all as he was engrossed in conversation with Armand, the warrior who had brought Angelique to them.

"Nadienne!" Angelique cried out, shrilly.

The woman's shoulders slumped as she turned back around, "*Oui,* mistress?"

"I want—"

Eyreka had heard enough. "Angelique," she said straightening her spine and placing her folded hands in her lap, hoping for an ounce of the serenity she strove to project, "one does not yell out one's wishes," she said quietly. "One must wait until the other person is within hearing distance before speaking."

Augustin cleared his throat loudly, but she ignored her husband and continued, "While you were resting this afternoon, Nadienne and Bernadette were unpacking your things. Then they unpacked their own. It would be impolite to expect that they would stay up until all hours when there are many others here who could easily serve."

Angelique's mouth had finally closed. Eyreka smiled inwardly. Obviously the little one needed a firmer hand. The determined look in Angelique's eyes told her that she had not been bested yet.

"I want Nadienne," she said, through clenched teeth.

"She is going to retire for the night. Should you need anything else, either myself, or one of my maidservants, will be more than happy to step in."

Eyreka turned away from the sputtering child, glancing at her husband. The flash of guilt in his expressive eyes confirmed that he would not gainsay her, but she knew they would speak of this later.

"Then I want Bernadette." Angelique announced loudly, crossing her arms in front of her little chest.

"Nadienne," Eyreka called out, "see that Bernadette retires with you," satisfied that her own dictate would be followed and the tired maids would go to bed.

But Angelique was not to be bested. "I want Simone," she shouted, pushing back away from the table, rising to her feet. "And I want her now!" she said, stamping her foot.

Augustin moved so fast Eyreka had little time to react. He placed his massive hands on his daughter's shoulders and bent down to whisper in her ear. Whatever he said, the child immediately relaxed and turned into his embrace. Augustin lifted her into his arms and strode from the room without a backward glance.

"She has been too long without a mother," Armand said

quietly.

Eyreka nodded, wondering if she would ever have peace in her household again.

EYREKA LAY IN the darkness, trying to decide how best to approach her new daughter. She turned on her side and closed her eyes. There was so much she wanted to talk over with Augustin, she sighed thinking of how distant he had become since the night in the herb garden. Thoughts of Augustin's mind-numbing kisses plagued her, while she drifted off to sleep.

"Eyreka."

The sound of her name being called disturbed her dreams. She waved a hand over her shoulder and turned away from the sound. The hand that clamped on her shoulder jarred her awake.

"What?" She sat up in bed, blinking at the brightness of the tallow candle her husband was setting down on the table by the bed.

"I need to speak with you," Augustin said quietly.

She looked up at him with one eye; the other was slow to cooperate. "It still hurts," she grumbled under her breath.

Augustin surprised her by sitting down on the bed and brushing the hair off of her forehead. "I must apologize for my daughter's actions earlier." He leaned forward and clasped his hands, resting them on his knees. "She is not usually such a disagreeable child," he said slowly.

"Truly?" Eyreka said, disbelief coloring her words.

Augustin gave her a hard look and shook his head.

"I see," she said carefully, "then she did not mean to blind me?"

The choked sound that Augustin made had her looking up at him. She narrowed her eyes, but he appeared concerned.

"Nay, I do not think that was her intent."

"Then she did not mean to render me lame?" she continued, trying to maintain her voice stern, when she really did want to laugh, now that she could look back at the little girl's attempts to make her will known.

Augustin chuckled before trying to cover it up with a cough.

"'Tis no use, I heard you laugh," she said in a hard voice.

"The look on your face was without price," he said smiling.

"I am sure knowing that will help me to see better on the morrow," she retorted.

Augustin's gaze met hers. "I will speak to her," he promised.

"As will I," Eyreka assured him. "I was afraid that you did not approve of the way I had spoken to her during our meal."

Augustin reached out and took her hands in his. A spark of awareness sizzled through her, startling her. Her gaze shot up and locked on his. His eyes were dark with passion.

"I thought that you—" she began.

"Why did you—" he said at the same time, then shook his head. "You first."

Eyreka was unsure of just how to broach the subject with her husband. She never had to ask Addison what he was thinking. She could read his thoughts with her heart. Would Augustin think her far too bold if she asked him to bed her? Was there a way she could ask without actually having to say the words?

At her silence, he squeezed her hands, "I promise not to laugh," he said quietly.

Eyreka gathered her courage and blurted out, "Why have you not touched me?"

Augustin dropped her hands and sat straighter. "I touched you just now. I brushed the hair off—"

"Not that way," she said miserably. "I know of no delicate way to say this, husband."

"Just say it then," he urged, his voice rough.

"Did you find our joining distasteful?" she asked in a small voice.

"*Mon Dieu.*" Augustin surged to his feet and began to pace. "Is that what you think?"

"What else can I think, when you have been avoiding me this fortnight past?"

Augustin pulled her to her feet and held on to her wrists. "Why did you pull back from me after I loved you?" he asked.

"I thought that you wanted me to."

After what sounded like a growl, he said, "I should have told you how I was feeling, but I was afraid that you regretted giving yourself to me."

"Just the opposite." She placed a finger to his lips. "I find that I am very distracted every time you walk into the room, and—"

Her words were cut off by his mouth. He kissed her with an intensity that she felt deep in her soul. All rational thought flew from her mind. She could not speak, but she could feel.

The warmth of his battled-hardened body seeped through her pores as she moaned in pleasure. Augustin's lips brushed down her neck.

"Let me look at you," he rasped. "I have waited long enough."

Eyreka's hands fell limply to her sides. Gathering her courage, she tilted her head and looked up at him, wondering whether or not she too should be so bold. Never one to sit back and let others lead the way, she decided…bold.

"So have I," she said, pulling his tunic over his head. Her breath caught in her throat, and she reached out to touch the jagged scar that nearly bisected his broad chest. The thick white line started beneath his collarbone and slashed across his breast, ending just above his left hip.

His eyes narrowed to slits of steely gray, and he started to pull back from her. Sensing his mood change, and sorry for it, she placed her lips on his collarbone and feathered a line of kisses along the uneven ridge of scar tissue.

"'Tis a horrible injury," she whispered. "You could have died." Eyreka knew without a doubt that a weaker man would have.

"Aye," he said, watching her.

Encouraged by the heat in his gaze, she started to run a fingertip across his chest, but what she saw stopped her cold. Sweat beaded on her upper lip. She closed her eyes and willed them to focus on what could not possibly be.

"What is wrong?" Augustin asked, cupping her cheek in his hand.

She opened her eyes and could not stop the tears, or her hand from reaching out to touch the small mark above Augustin's heart.

"'Tis no grievous injury," he assured her, "but a mark I have had from birth."

Eyreka caught herself beginning to trace an X on the mark. "My husband had such a mark," she whispered raggedly.

"A coincidence," he murmured.

"Nay," she said with conviction, "mayhap fate."

"A birthmark?" he chided her.

"My husband died when a Norman arrow pierced his heart." She looked up at him, expecting anger or disdain, but the compassion and understanding in his gaze were her undoing.

"Where did he die?" Augustin asked.

"Not ten miles from Merewood."

"When?" he urged.

"Three years past."

"Do you think me responsible?" he asked in a rough voice.

Eyreka shook her head. "How could you possibly know the faces of the men you have killed?"

Augustin pulled her against him and dropped his chin to rest on the top of her head. "There are many I don't even see in the heat of battle," he admitted. "But there are the faces of those I have battled, who fought bravely and died bravely. I will carry their memory to my grave."

"Were you here three years ago?" She hated having to ask, and dreaded hearing the answer.

"Aye," he answered honestly. "I could have given the order to fire the arrow that took his life."

As he held her close, the rhythmic beating of his heart soothed her. Augustin could have lied, but he did not. He could be responsible for Addison's death.

She struggled to concentrate on what Augustin had said, his honesty. While he continued to hold her close and soothe her, she realized that finding the man who'd taken her husband's life during a battle to secure the Norman's hold over her people would be pointless.

Addison willingly gave his life for what he believed in, freedom to live the Saxon way of life. Could she hate Augustin for wanting to do the same? He was part of the future of Merewood Keep, mayhap her destiny. She knew that she must reach out with an open heart and trusting soul.

Later, snuggled close to Augustin's warmth, comforted by his touch, she drew in a breath and let go of her pride. With her husband's arms wrapped around her, Eyreka breathed in a contented sigh and drifted off to sleep.

CHAPTER TWENTY

EYREKA WOKE WITH the feeling that something was not right. She rolled over onto her stomach, brushed the hair out of her face and propped her elbows beneath her. Looking around the room, all seemed to be in order, then she remembered... Augustin.

Heat rose in her cheeks thinking of the way they had spent the night locked in each other's arms. A curl of heat spiraled through her as she remembered each touch, each taste of ecstasy they had shared. Sometime during the night she had lost a part of herself, and feared that she would never be whole without it. Touching the empty spot next to her, she smiled; it was still warm where her husband had lain.

He had risen without waking her and gone. How long would it be before he would begin to share his thoughts with her, tell her of his plans as her first husband had?

The early morning discussions to plan the day was a special time that she missed most of all. The sharing of future plans and dreams for the future forged a bond between husband and wife that grew stronger with the years. She ached to share those plans and dreams with Augustin.

The warmth of the sun radiated through the arrowslit, tempting her to rise and greet the day. The early morning sounds of the holding waking were comforting. Mayhap she should check on

Angelique. Eyreka silently wondered what delightful surprises the little one had in store for her today. She would definitely have to keep her wits about her, or she would lose the battle to win the little tyrant over.

"I WANT THE land," de Jeaneaux said evenly, watching for a reaction from the man sitting across from him. "De Chauret would never have received the offer if he had not taken my place in the king's regard." De Jeaneaux paused, "The land should have been deeded to me."

Aaron the Saxon closed his hand around the razor-sharp edge of his dagger. A thin line of bright red blood ran down his wrist. He handed the dagger to de Jeaneaux. "We seal our bargain in blood."

De Jeaneaux accepted the blade and did the same.

Aaron's voice rasped, "I can forego the land. I still have control over Sedgeworth in Owen's absence, but I want the woman." He vowed through gritted teeth, "She will be made to pay for interfering in my liege's plans for his former ward, Jillian of Loughmae. Because of Eyreka, Milord Owen awaits a death sentence … mayhap even one of treason."

Bloody hands clasped, their gazes met and held until de Jeaneaux nodded in agreement.

"I DO NOT see why I cannot ride out alone," Angelique said, sticking her bottom lip out in a full-fledged pout worthy of her ten years.

Augustin shook his head. "There is much you do not know of the countryside."

At her watery sniff, he turned back toward his daughter.

BARGAINING WITH THE LADY OF MEREWOOD

"When have you ridden out alone in the past?"

Angelique looked at her feet as if she found them fascinating. Undeterred by her reluctance to answer him, he tilted her chin up so that he could see her mutinous expression.

"Whenever it pleased me," she finally answered, crossing her arms in front of her.

It was a posture vaguely familiar, though at the moment, he could not recall why. "Now that you are here, you are subject to the same rules as the other women under my protection."

"I do not like rules, or her." Angelique eyes blazed with anger.

"You will come to like Lady Eyreka," Augustin said without pause, amazed that once he said the words, they were exactly true. He had come to like Eyreka, very much.

"I will not," his daughter said quietly, with all of the heartfelt conviction her little soul possessed.

"Can you not open your heart, just a little?" he prodded. When she shook her head no, he sighed. "Try."

"Good morning, husband," Eyreka said, walking into the hall. When he turned toward her, time seemed to grind to a halt and everyone in the room faded into the background, until it was just the two of them facing one another across the vast expanse of the hall.

Heat curled low in his gut and started to spread to his limbs, reminding him of the passion that had burned between them last night.

He strode purposefully toward her, took her hand in his and pressed his mouth against the back of it, though he wanted to press his lips over her heart. Thinking of doing just that, he wondered what would happen if he surprised his wife with a gentle reminder of what they had shared. His gaze turned mischievous as he flipped her hand over and placed a fervent kiss in the palm of her hand. Eyreka jolted, then blushed a becoming shade of pink, when he touched the center of her palm with the tip of his tongue.

Her knees nearly gave out, and would have, had he not steadied her with both hands. The knowledge that he could affect her thusly swept through him. "You slept well?" he dared to ask, though he knew very well neither of them slept.

Eyreka nodded absently, staring at their still-joined hands. Taking her by the elbow, he escorted her over to the table and motioned for the young man holding a tray filled with food to serve them.

"Papa," Angelique said, in a loud voice, "I want to go riding this morning."

Eyreka looked over at her...the girl had obviously braided her own hair. It was lopsided, with strands of hair pulling free of the ribbon she had used to secure it in place. She wondered if one of the maidservants had offered to help, then decided that they hadn't. She had not seen either of them since the evening before when she sent them to bed.

"How about a tour of your new home?" Eyreka offered, hoping to catch Angelique off balance with her offer.

"Who would take me?" Angelique asked, leaning forward past her father.

"I am free this morning," Eyreka said.

"In that case, *ma petite*," Augustin answered smoothly, "you may accompany Lady Eyreka."

Augustin's daughter rose from the table like an arrow loosed from a taut bowstring. "I'd rather work on my sewing."

Augustin laughed aloud. "But you hate to sew."

The implication was not lost on Eyreka. She nodded slowly, accepting the girl's choice. But she was not easily defeated. "I will see that you have the threads you need," she told her quietly. "Sara will be happy to show Nadienne and Bernadette around the grounds today," she paused, hoping to draw Angelique's attention.

"And what will you do," the little one finally asked, her tone far too sweet-sounding for the sour look that lined her little face.

"I shall ride out today. 'Tis far too beautiful a day to waste

BARGAINING WITH THE LADY OF MEREWOOD

indoors."

Augustin shook his head. "It is not safe," he said simply.

Eyreka struggled not to snip at him, knowing he was concerned, but surely those that had been bent on doing her harm were gone. "You and my sons have taken care of any problems of infidels. There should not be any left." She silently begged him with her gaze to relent and let her ride.

Augustin looked thoughtful and seemed to be swaying in her direction.

"I can take a company of armed men as protection. No one will catch us by surprise."

Finally, he nodded. "Take extra men," he warned.

"Thank you. I shall so enjoy the ride," she said.

Augustin flashed her a quick grin, obviously pleased with the way she handled the latest confrontation with his daughter. Eyreka rose from the table and nodded toward her husband, "If you will excuse me."

"I want to ride, Papa," Angelique wailed.

"Then I suggest you catch up to Lady Eyreka and apologize."

Eyreka smiled to herself, pausing at the door, making a great show of brushing imaginary crumbs from her skirts. A whisper of sound told her that her stepdaughter was right behind her. She turned around and placed a hand to her breast, "Oh," she said as if shocked, "you startled me."

Angelique's eyes narrowed as if she didn't believe her, but Eyreka maintained her startled look.

"I am sorry for being rude," Angelique said haltingly. "I would rather go riding with you."

Contentment filled Eyreka, as she ran the tip of her forefinger down the little girl's nose. "I'm glad."

The girl didn't shrug away from her, but stood still, permitting Eyreka to touch her. Then she nodded and walked along beside her. A silent truce had been formed with the girl's apology. It was a beginning.

Patrick raised a hand as he crossed the lower bailey. Eyreka smiled, waved back at him and continued walking toward the stable.

"Who is he?" Angelique asked, her eyes widening at the size of the redheaded warrior.

"Patrick. He's one of my son's vassals."

"You have a son?"

Eyreka smiled, "I have three."

"Three?" Angelique said surprised. "How old are they?"

Eyreka took her by the arm, steering her clear of a fresh pile of manure directly in front of them.

"Garrick, my eldest, is five and twenty, Dunstan is—"

Angelique's gasp of horror was almost funny, "You must be ancient!"

Eyreka flushed scarlet at the comment, indignation rising in her breast, but one look at the little girl's face and she had to laugh. "Aye." They walked the rest of the way in silence, with Angelique sneaking glances at her every few moments.

Her horse saddled and ready to ride, Eyreka led the way, leaving her stepdaughter to follow along with ten men at arms. The echoing sound of hoof beats pounding the softly packed dirt of the bailey told her that Angelique had not wasted any time.

A companionable silence settled between them as they rode across lush green grass, skirted sparkling ponds, and rode between majestic pines. Eyreka approved of Angelique's hushed tone when the little girl admitted, grudgingly, that their land was truly wondrous.

Shouts off in the distance echoed toward them on the mid-morning breeze. The unmistakable sound of sword striking sword sliced through their calm. Armand held up a hand, signaling for silence, and motioned for one of the other warriors to ride up ahead to see what had happened.

While they waited, Angelique sidled her mount closer to Eyreka's. Without thinking, Eyreka laid a calming hand on the other horse's neck, whispering words to soothe the anxious animal.

"He likes you."

Eyreka ignored the girl's surprise, "I feed him bits of apple from our orchard." It was a good sign that Angelique was observant. Mayhap she could use it to her advantage in helping the child accept her new situation.

"Did he ever bite you?" Angelique asked, lowering her voice.

Eyreka stroked the horse's velvety muzzle. "More than once, the rascal."

"But you still feed him?" the child persisted. "Aren't you afraid he'll bite you again?"

"If I am careful, he will not take me by surprise again, if I'm not ..." she let her words trail off, watching as the warrior rode back toward their group at a furious pace.

"'Tis the patrol," he said, gasping for breath. "They've been attacked."

At his words the two other knights looked over at the women and stiffened noticeably. Armand spoke, "We must get Lady Eyreka and Angelique to safety." The other men agreed, closing rank to form a protective human shield around Eyreka and her charge. The look in Armand's eyes chilled her to the bone.

"Mayhap we should wait here while you and the others offer your support." She hoped the Norman warrior would not disagree; time could be of the essence.

Armand's face darkened.

"Are they evenly matched?" she asked, hoping to push the warrior into agreeing with her.

"They are outnumbered," he rasped.

"The sooner you add to their number, the sooner we can all ride back to safety," she reasoned.

Angelique looked at Eyreka as if she had grown another head, but blessedly remained quiet.

"Augustin will have my bones stripped clean and hang them out to bleach in the sun," Armand repeated with such passion, Eyreka wondered if that was not an oft-used threat to ensure the younger warriors in line.

"I cannot imagine that he would truly wish to," she answered. "Can you not see the advantage?"

Armand's hands shook in frustration as he stared toward the sounds of battle. "He will kill me," he said quietly.

"We promise not to tell," Angelique implored, her blue eyes shining.

At his reluctant nod, Eyreka drew her small, but lethal-looking dagger from the leather sheath that hung from her waist, and slid from her horse. Putting a hand to her lips she led both horses into the dense bushes that lined the road and waited.

"Will Armand be all right?" Angelique whispered brokenly.

Compassion filled Eyreka's breast at her concern, "He is a strong warrior," she said softly. "He will be fine."

The wait seemed interminable, and it was a long while after the sounds of battle diminished that Eyreka could finally hear the sound of approaching horses. With Augustin's daughter behind her, she stood feet spread and dagger at the ready.

"Lady Eyreka!"

Armand's cry had her re-sheathing her weapon. She called over her shoulder, "They are back." She waited until the warriors drew up alongside their hiding place before revealing herself. The boast that she had needed no protection from the warriors died on her lips. The group of men before her seemed to be awash in blood. The high-pitched scream that rent the air had her spinning around, grabbing Angelique with firm hands. She pulled the child into her embrace, whispering words in a bid to calm her.

"Armand needs me," she told the child in clipped tones. "And I need you to help me bind their wounds."

Chapter Twenty-One

"Milady!" Aimory called out as the group rode through Merewood's massive wood gate.

Eyreka raised her head toward the sound of his voice. The look on Aimory's face made her sigh with resignation. Worry lined his brow, while tension seemed to stiffen the muscles of his body. It was time to have a private talk with him, but it would bear careful consideration first. Raising sons had made her very aware of just how great the need to hold onto their young pride truly was. She hoped that her husband had not seen the look in the young knight's gaze, he was bound to misunderstand.

"Angelique!" Augustin called out, striding across the lower bailey, dodging a young lad diligently shoveling horse manure onto a cart already heaped with soiled straw from the stables.

He paused to look over his shoulder, "You've a fine rhythm going, Owen," he encouraged. "Remember to bend your knees when you lift."

Eyreka had to smile at the look on the young man's face. She knew from his bemused look that he had not expected their Norman Lord to be aware that he existed, let alone praise him for performing the meanest of jobs. Her first husband had, though. Addison had made a point of knowing everyone's name and had performed all of the tasks, oft-times while the younger of their household watched. Their sons had grown up knowing their father was not too proud to shovel steaming piles of horse dung.

That the new lord of the keep showed similar tendencies made all of the recent upheaval and difficulties worthwhile.

Angelique scooted down off the back of her horse and threw herself into her father's waiting arms. Eyreka watched the look of relief soften his features as he drew his precious child to his breast, enfolding her in steely bands of protectiveness. Longing to be held just that way caught her off guard.

She reached for the bit of amber that hung around her neck, blindly feeling for the carved inscriptions. The prophecy of a strong warrior coming to protect the wearer in times of need made her smile. So far her rescuers had come after she had been forced to defend herself. Her thoughts turned toward Garrick's wife and the odds Jillian had battled against to survive. I must return her necklace today, she thought.

"Ahh, *ma petite*," Augustin said, drawing back from the little girl. "You have had more than your share of adventure this day."

She nodded and looked over at Eyreka, "Lady Eyreka is a skilled healer."

Without another word, the young girl walked over to where the injured Armand was still holding her mount. *"Merci,* Armand," she said politely.

The shock on the man's face told Eyreka that it was not the way her new daughter usually acted. The warrior bent down on one knee, so that he was eye level with his tiny mistress, and solemnly replied, "You are most welcome, *ange.*"

Eyreka sincerely doubted that Angelique was an angel at all, but was not about to say so and destroy the moment of revelation for the hardened warrior. Who was she to say that the little girl was not pleasant to everyone else but her? After all, 'twas not as if she herself would be amenable to another woman trying to replace her mother. Eyreka doubted she would have been as calm as Angelique.

She shook her head sadly, knowing she would have tried to slip something cold and slimy between the interloper's bed linens or mayhap something with many legs into the woman's evening trencher. She had used both tricks herself to get her father's attention after her own mother died.

A sense of understanding filled her as she watched the girl side-step the young lad still mucking the bailey, and dance up the steps to the hall, twirling around the two maidservants who waited to be summoned. The young had the startling ability to block out the horrors life threw in their path. Mayhap it was a blessing, she thought. Recovering her poise, she called out to one of the serving maids that hovered at the base of the steps and asked her to fetch Sara.

The one end of the hall looked like it had in the aftermath of the bloody siege more than twenty winters ago. As Eyreka worked to sew and re-bind the warriors' wounds, Angelique helped.

"Sara!" she called out, grateful when the woman placed yet another bowl of warm, herb-scented water by her elbow. The used bloody bowl was removed, and another stack of linen strips was placed within reach. Eyreka took a moment to step back from the ragged gash she stitched to stretch her aching back. She was not used to working so intently for such a long period of time, thank the gods, not since Merewood Keep had fallen.

Augustin's touch surprised her. She jumped, dropping a clean strip of linen onto the soiled rushes at her feet. He bent down to retrieve it for her, but she stopped him, "Nay, I cannot use it now, it would cause Henri's wound to fester."

"Why?" Augustin asked intrigued.

"I do not know, other than the fact that after years of learning the art of healing at my mother's elbow, and watching the men who caught wound-fever and died," she said in a low voice, "there seemed to be a commonality among the ones who died so soon after being cared for."

Her husband's interest was definitely centered on what she said. His gaze was narrowed, and he seemed to be concentrating on every word.

"The wounds that were painstakingly cleansed, even those without healing herbs, did not fester as badly as the ones that were simply bound up and left to heal."

Henri poked her shoulder with his meaty forefinger. "Have you washed it out then?"

His question made her smile. "Aye, though you'll have to come back and let me change the bandage again in the morning," she told him, winding the linen securely around the warrior's arm.

He eyed her with what she guessed was speculation. It was the truth, she knew he did not trust her, but at least he had come to appreciate her skills and had stopped questioning her every move.

The older man nodded and rose to leave. As she wiped her hands dry, he called to her, "*Merci*, milady," he said gruffly.

Augustin mumbled something under his breath and followed his vassal out of the hall. Eyreka knew that the time for questions had begun. Henri was the last of the patrol to be seen to. Though his wound was the most serious, he had insisted that she take care of the others first.

Eyreka gathered the soiled linens and piled them together; they would need to be laundered two times before they were fit to be used again. All of Augustin's men are honorable and trustworthy, she thought watching the group move off to go about their varied duties. Why then could they not give their loyalty to her as she so willingly gave it to them?

"My husband is an honorable man," she said aloud.

"'Tis the only reason I have struggled to convince people not to rise against him," Garrick said quietly.

"I did not know you were there." Eyreka did not like being caught unaware.

"If you had known, you would not have revealed your true thoughts," he chided.

Eyreka mulled over her son's words, relieved that he would readily admit what was in his heart.

"What happened out there?" she asked, changing the subject, hoping for a direct answer.

"Henri headed up the dawn patrol," her son said, a frown beginning to form a crease between his brows. "They were attacked on their way back from the southern meadow."

"Did they recognize any of the warriors?"

Garrick's look made her laugh.

"I suppose all Saxons look the same to our Norman guards, do they not?" she said softly.

"So I have heard," he answered. "Jean said that they had found evidence of two more encampments, both in the wood that borders the southern meadow."

"It would bear investigating." Eyreka lowered her voice. She did not want anyone to hear their hushed conversation.

"So you don't know?" Garrick looked surprised.

"Know what?" Eyreka demanded, placing her hands on her hips.

"Mayhap you should ask your husband."

"Mayhap I will add some herbs to your evening meal," Eyreka said evenly. "Ones that are guaranteed to cramp your belly."

"For the love of God, Mother," Garrick said, trying to control his anger.

"Tell me," she urged, knowing he would not dare refuse her.

"For the past week, each patrol has reported similar findings ... abandoned encampments."

"And?"

"These last two would indicate that someone has camped in a circle around Merewood. As if they were watching our holding from all angles."

"To best decide our weakest point?"

To her dismay, Garrick nodded. "'Twould be my guess. You'll have to ask Augustin to be certain."

She clenched her hands at her sides and started to walk away. Garrick's hand on her arm stopped her. "There is more," he admitted.

She could sense whatever it was devastated her son. "Tell me," she implored.

"Our grain," he said haltingly, "has been trampled."

Before anyone could stop her, Eyreka ran out of the hall and was in the stables saddling her own mount. She had to ride out to view the devastation firsthand.

The sight of the nearly grown green plants lying flat on the ground had a lump of anguish forming in her throat. What would her people eat? The sound of hoof beats galloping up behind her broke through her troubled thoughts. She dashed the tears from her cheeks. Looking over her shoulder, she saw the anguish in Garrick's tortured gaze. Before she could speak, Dunstan arrived with five warriors.

"Who would do such a thing?" She dismounted and knelt down to touch the trampled grain, disbelief warring with the need for answers. "What have you done about this?" she demanded of her sons.

Garrick shifted from one foot to the other and glared at her. "I have reported the damage to the lord of the keep," he bit out. "Your husband has sent a patrol of men out to track down whoever is behind this atrocity."

"Do we have enough grain stored to feed our people?" she asked Dunstan, hesitatingly. When he nodded, she continued, "What about for planting?"

"Aye, but we must replant immediately," Dunstan looked out over the vast field of trampled grain.

"If I had the time or manpower, I would have planted all of the seed," he said slowly. "If I had—" Dunstan left the thought unfinished, but she knew what he was going to say ... they would have lost the entire crop, the king would not have received his share of the revenue, and their people would once again be in danger of starving.

"Who could possibly want to see our people suffer again?" she demanded. Her anger filled her with the need to act.

Garrick's eyes narrowed as he stared off in the distance. As she watched, her son's jaw clenched and his mouth formed a thin line of grim determination, "Garrick," she prompted.

"Dunstan, escort Mother back," he ordered.

"I do not wish—"

Garrick turned around and ground out, "I do not have time to be concerned with your wishes."

Eyreka started to reply, but was cut off when Garrick continued, "You did not heed our wishes when you wed de Chauret." His face flushed with anger. "If you had, we could have told you something like this would happen."

"I…don't understand," she stammered.

"Aye, Mother, you do not," he bit out. "The Saxon people have been taken over by the Normans, and our attempts to rise up against the Conqueror have failed. Not everyone has learned to accept that the Normans are here to stay, as I have."

"There are those who would see de Chauret fail," Dunstan added.

"But our people would starve!" she answered, indignant.

"And their traitorous mistress with them," Garrick answered.

"Do you think I have betrayed our people?" she rasped, pain slicing through her heart at the coldness behind her son's words.

Garrick shook his head, "Nay, but I would have rather left Merewood than see you wed to a Norman."

Dunstan nodded his agreement.

"What is done, cannot be undone," she said, straightening her spine and gritting her teeth. "I have done what I thought was best for our people."

Garrick grimaced, "Let us hope the retaliation will end here," he said in a low voice.

As Eyreka and Dunstan rode away, Patrick leaned toward Garrick, steadying his fractious mount. "Owen?" he asked.

Garrick shook his head, "He is still in London awaiting trial."

"Who then?" Kelly asked, moving his mount in between the two warriors.

Patrick and Garrick's gazes met and held. "Aaron?"

"I thought he was dead," Kelly said in a quiet voice.

"I thought so, too," Patrick answered.

"Will we have to tell Augustin about him?" Kelly asked.

"Not until we have more proof," Garrick answered.

His mother and brother were mere specks in the distance when he finally spurred his destrier to follow them. His gut roiled as fear clashed with anger. The women he loved were still in danger.

⟫⟫⟨⟨

"IS THERE ENOUGH to plant another crop?" Augustin could not believe the worry over the trampled plants. He was on edge, agitated. He disliked having to worry about something he did not understand. You could not hold grain in your hand like a weapon, therefore, he reasoned, he did not need to know how to sow it, tend it, or reap it.

"The king will not receive his full share if we are to feed Merewood's people," Dunstan answered.

"Let me worry about William's share," Augustin said calmly. "He is not without reason."

Dunstan snorted, but held back whatever he was about to say at Augustin's hard look.

"Do you need extra men to plant the crop?" Augustin asked.

"Nay," Dunstan said, shaking his head, "mayhap to guard it."

Augustin nodded, relieved that Dunstan would see to the chore. The sudden thought that Eyreka's sons were capable of running the holding without him bothered him. Garrick had the head for planning the defense of it, while Dunstan had the heart for ensuring their people were fed. In his bid to please his king and accept the offered holding, he hadn't thought beyond making his mark upon these people, confident that only he and his personal guard could run the holding. He began to wonder how he would integrate these two peoples without compromising the way Merewood Keep had been thriving.

Eyreka served their people well, mayhap too well. Thinking of his wife, he smiled. She was never in one spot long, unless it was time for a meal, he grumbled to himself. A dark thought filled him ... he was not needed here. On the heels of that thought came another. Eyreka did not need him either. Shaking his head to rid himself of that thought, he frowned. He was Lord of Merewood, his wife and their people would come to rely on him.

EYREKA WAITED UNTIL she and Augustin were alone in their chamber before she confronted him with her fears. Augustin's eyes had taken on the familiar look she had come to watch for, one filled with hunger. But she refused to let herself be swayed by his nearness. She pushed out of his arms and blurted out, "Are we being attacked?"

While she watched, Augustin's eyes changed to a lighter shade of gray. The look of hunger was replaced with a look of speculation. "Do you see hails of arrows raining down upon the warriors guarding the curtain wall?"

She shook her head, "Nay, but—"

"Do you see a siege tower butted up against the outside our thick stone walls?" he continued.

"Nay, but—"

"Then why would you ask such a question?" he demanded.

"The campfires," she said simply, hoping her husband would volunteer information.

"What campfires?" he asked, watching her with cold clear eyes.

Anger filled her. There was nowhere she could go to escape the hurt feelings that wrapped tightly about her breast, squeezing her. "I thought we had come to an understanding," she whispered.

His look warmed as his gaze raked her from head to toe. "We have." He reached for her.

Eyreka spun about so that he could not grab her and pull her to him. She would not let him addle her wits with the heat of his touch. "What we have is desire and passion," she said brokenly, "nothing more." She inched backward until she could feel the rough wooden planks of the chamber door beneath her hands.

"You agreed." His voice took on an edge of steel, as he stalked closer.

"And I am ten times a fool," she said, opening the door and slipping through. Her swift footsteps carried her down to the lower level and through the now empty hall. She did not stop until she had reached the corner of the herb garden.

A whisper of sound told her that she had not succeeded in eluding the man she married. She refused to think of him as her husband. Nay, she thought, a husband would be considerate of her feelings. A husband would expect a helpmate in all things ... he would trust her enough to confide important matters, like the random campsites surrounding their holding.

He is not Addison, a voice seemed to echo through her tired brain.

"I am not Addison," Augustin bit out.

Rough hands upon her shoulders spun her about to face him. Anger seeped through his fingertips until she could feel the imprint she knew would be a telltale purple mark tomorrow.

She wanted to rant and rave. She wanted to push him and shove him on his arrogant backside. But she had not the strength. Caring for his men had drained what little energy remained. She felt her shoulders slump, as if they could no longer support the weight of his hands.

Augustin's grip immediately loosened. "I do not understand why."

"Aye," she agreed. "Mayhap I should not have hoped for what I had in the past."

"And that would be?" he rasped, dropping his hands to his sides.

"There was naught that my husband kept from me," she said slowly. "He did not withhold crucial happenings from me, for fear that I would not understand their significance." She flinched, her voice sounded bitter to her own ears.

"Why would he confide his worries in you?" he asked, the tone of his voice sounding amazed. "'Tis a husband's place to protect his wife."

It was then she knew he did not understand that very reason she needed to be a part of his day. She needed to hear that there was trouble surrounding their home, and needed to be asked for her thoughts on handling the situation.

She gathered what little strength was left and tried to make him understand. "I was not much older than your daughter when I accompanied my father on his planned siege of Merewood Keep."

Augustin's attention was centered on her, his gaze had sharpened. He took her by the hand and led her over to a wide flat stone and helped her to sit. He then sat beside her, waiting.

Words spilled from her lips as she told of her father's ill-fated siege. His eyes narrowed as he listened to her explain how her Viking father had laid siege to Merewood, while a force of Danes had managed to block their retreat. Augustin had thought her to be Saxon by blood ... not by marriage.

"There was naught else to do but offer to help the Saxons defend Merewood against the larger group of Danish invaders or be slaughtered."

"Did he die?"

"Not that day," she said shaking her head. "The Lord of Merewood was young and arrogant...ruthless...but not without brains. He accepted our offer of defense, thus tripling the number of warriors protecting Merewood."

"And in exchange?" Augustin urged.

"In exchange, my father's warriors would have the food and

water they needed, along with the protection of the walls of Merewood Keep, until the Danes were vanquished."

She must have hesitated long enough for Augustin to catch on that there was more to the story. Unable to finish the tale, she rose to her feet and brushed out her skirts.

She had not taken two steps when he hauled her around to face him and demanded, "Finish it."

"While they battled the Danes, Siguird's daughter had to remain in the hall to ensure his allegiance. Until the battle was over, no Vikings were allowed entrance to the hall or inner bailey, where the food stores and well were located."

"Did your father have more than one daughter?" Augustin asked, his voice rough with emotion.

Eyreka shook her head.

Augustin enfolded her in his strong embrace. She allowed herself to be soothed. As he fell silent, she guessed that his mind would be trying to piece together the rest of the story. The night air carried a sudden chill as she realized that he would think ill of her first husband if she did not tell him all of it.

"The battle was long and bloody," she continued, "with many dead on both sides. During that time, I had grown used to Addison's presence. As I watched how he treated his own people, I realized, not only was he a skilled warrior, but also a fair and honorable man ... like my own father."

Augustin did not speak, but the understanding look in his eyes warmed her.

"When the wounded had been patched up, and I could see the uncertainty that plagued the Saxons of Merewood and my people, I made a bold decision. I offered to remain as wife to Addison of Merewood in exchange for freedom for my father and our people."

"Your father allowed you to speak?"

"Aye," she said softly, "he knew there was no use in trying to deny me."

"And Addison?"

"I was very skilled as a healer even then. I had saved more than one of Addison's warriors, and he was yet unmarried and very grateful."

"I see."

"We grew to love one another. We shared that love with our children. It was a good life ... I miss him." she paused, drew in a deep, fortifying breath and continued. "I would do anything for my family, Augustin." Her voice was firm, "But I would never act without honor."

Walking away from the silent man, Eyreka realized that while similar, the circumstances leading to their marriage were not the same. Merewood was not under siege, and the Danes were not bearing down upon them. Random encampments had been discovered, but Augustin's men would flush out whomever watched Merewood's walls. There was no danger of her having to put herself in the middle again.

CHAPTER TWENTY-TWO

GARRICK AND AUGUSTIN had taken to riding out on patrol together. It pleased Eyreka to see Garrick's stiff-necked pride give way to grudging admiration for her husband. Her eldest had finally let go of his hatred of Normans long enough to glimpse the man beneath the warrior's facade.

She noticed Dunstan seeking Augustin out more and more, as the damaged crop had been cleared and a new one planted. Though Augustin did not seem to be able to offer any suggestions as to how to proceed, she noticed he did offer his whole-hearted support of Dunstan's decisions. Augustin was intelligent enough to realize Dunstan's value, and did not try to wrest control out of the younger man's capable hands.

She smiled to herself, knowing for a fact that Augustin would rather be bested by the quintain, and face the jeers of his men, than tally up their spices, or barrels of meat and grain. He was more than happy to leave that to Dunstan.

Though she was loath to do it, she had spoken to Aimory, gently explaining how she felt about her husband. Aimory accepted her words with quiet dignity. She liked him better for it.

A feeling of peace pervaded their lives. Eyreka reveled in it, thinking that at long last she had achieved her goal uniting their two peoples.

"A soak in a hot tub would relieve the ache," she heard

Georges grumble as he and Augustin entered the hall.

She walked over to where they stood arguing. Both men were covered in a layer of sweat and grime. "Planting again, husband?" she teased, pleased by the flash of desire that darkened his gaze.

"Hah!" Georges grunted. "Doesn't know when to give up," he said cryptically, walking away.

"Sara, have hot water brought to the bathing chamber," Eyreka called out. The maidservant nodded and went to do as she was bid.

"I have to speak to Georges," Augustin rasped while staring pointedly at her lips. She touched her fingertips to them, feeling the caress in his gaze.

"I'll be waiting," she promised.

She set out bowls holding lighted tallow-fat candles and smaller ones with fragrant lavender. Nervous, she grabbed a handful of the dried blossoms and crushed them in her fist.

"Going to add that to the water?" Sara asked, tilting her head to one side as if waiting for Eyreka's response.

"I think the lavender and mint soap will do." Eyreka ignored Sara's pointed look.

"Is there anything—" Sara started to say.

"That will be all for now," Eyreka interrupted, smoothing the stack of drying cloths. "Thank you."

Sara nodded and opened the door to leave. "Milord."

"Sara." Watching her hasty retreat, he asked, "Is there a problem? She seemed to be in a hur—" The words stuck in his throat as his gaze swept the room, centering on the silver maiden wreathed in the soft glow of candle flame.

"Let me help you," Eyreka offered, dragging the tunic up and over his head.

Augustin felt his control slip a notch and desperately tried to hang on to it.

Eyreka beckoned, and he followed to the side of the tub. She helped him remove his braies. He was not a vain man, he knew his body was a mass of scars, but the way Eyreka stared at him made him feel invincible. Her eyes darkened as her gaze caressed the width of his shoulders and slid across the taut muscles of his abdomen.

"*Mon Dieu*," he groaned.

She seemed to come back to her senses at his uttered oath. "I'll get the soap." Eyreka turned away, and he slipped into the tub, afraid his wife's hungry gaze would weaken his knees to the point where he would fall on his face.

She poured warm water over his back and shoulders and worked up a lather in her hands, before sliding them across the knotted muscles in his upper back. He relaxed under the continuous hypnotic movement. Her hands slid over his shoulders, down across his back, and then up and around again.

"Mmm," she breathed.

Caught up in the web of pleasure her hands wove, Augustin leaned back against the tub and closed his eyes. Eyreka slipped her soapy hands across his collarbones, kneading his pectoral muscles.

"Let me wash your hair." Eyreka thought she heard a catch in his breathing, but was concentrating on the pure pleasure of sinking her hands into his thick chestnut waves. She'd wanted to touch his hair since that first day.

Slowly, she worked up a lather, massaging his scalp down to the nape of his neck and back up to his forehead. He started to sit up, but she pushed him back down. "You'll get soap in your beautiful eyes."

"Lady, I have been called many things," Augustin said huskily, "but never that."

She rinsed his hair and set the bucket alongside the tub. "Never?"

Despite the fact that his body was crisscrossed with scars, Augustin was a beautiful man. Power and heat radiated from him. His gray-streaked waves were a warm, rich brown, with but a hint of red fire.

She shook her head. "An oversight, milord," she whispered, "one that I find hard to believe."

As he drew her into the tub, Eyreka's eyes locked with his. Something deeper than desire burned there. His loneliness called out to her as his soul-deep pain held her captive.

She was afraid she was living proof that the Viking prophecy was true ... she was falling in love with her husband.

He claimed her in a mind-numbing kiss that had her fear melting away. Augustin's lips slid across her cheek and nibbled a path along the sensitized skin of her jaw.

"Hotter than the fires," she whimpered, leaning back against the tub, "that forged Thor's hammer."

Gathering her close to his heart, he stood on quaking legs, lifting her from the tub. Gently setting her on the bench, he wrapped a drying cloth about his waist and then wrapped another around Eyreka, drawing her to her feet. A familiar feeling of contentment was spreading through him. *Mon Dieu*, he was falling in love with his wife.

He dressed quickly and bundled her in his arms, carrying her back to their chamber. He smiled, thinking of how he was becoming accustomed to the feel of her womanly curves, her own special scent of lavender and rain, and her smiles. The change had been abrupt, and he was man enough to admit it to himself that he wasn't falling in love with his wife...he *was* in love with her.

"BUT I WANT to ride now!" Angelique said, stamping her foot for emphasis.

Eyreka sighed, it was obviously to be her day for interruptions.

"I am busy." She had to finish decanting the now cooled liquid she had extracted from the crushed foxglove.

"Mayhap later this afternoon," she offered, finishing her task and looking up. The girl's braid was coming apart, and her chainse and bliaut looked as if she had slept in them. Startled by the change in Angelique's normally neat appearance, Eyreka brushed her hands on the sides of her gown and walked over to the open doorway where the little one stood.

Taking a chance that Angelique would not brush her off, she asked, "Who helped you to dress this morn?"

Angelique's entire body stiffened, and her little chin came up. "I don't need help," she announced haughtily, her ice-blue eyes flashing a warning to those who would suggest she did.

For a brief moment, Eyreka debated whether or not to heed it. She decided she was not quite up to doing battle a second time that day, her sons had drained her fighting spirit. Her relationship with Angelique, if you could call it such, was too new ... emotions too tenuous, she decided to go carefully.

"Mayhap you misunderstand me."

Angelique's expressive face mirrored the confusion Eyreka was certain lay just beneath the calm facade the girl chose to show the world.

She took pity on the little one and explained, "When one is mistress of an important holding, such as Merewood Keep, there are servants who are ready to assist their mistress in all things."

Angelique nodded, waiting for her to continue.

"It is up to the lady of the keep to decide when and where she requires that assistance."

"My father needs no help." The challenge was blatant.

"I am sure that he does not, but a wise master knows when to seek help out of necessity, and when to seek help to allow those of his people to be an active part in the life of their home."

Eyreka knew her stepdaughter was considering this bit of insight very carefully. The little one's brow was deeply furrowed, while she kicked at the newly laid rushes with the toe of her boot.

She took a step closer. Thankfully the little girl did not shy away this time. Encouraged, she spoke in a quiet voice, "My mother used to rinse my hair with chamomile flowers and honeysuckle."

Angelique looked up at her and countered, "Genvieve says that elder flowers and walnut leaves are what raven-wing tresses need."

"Raven-wing." Eyreka smiled. "How lovely." She could not stop herself, she reached out with her right hand and stroked the top of Angelique's dark head. "'Tis like my river stones, so very smooth."

Angelique grumbled under her breath, but she stayed put. Eyreka sensed the girl's resistance slowly ebbing away.

"Genvieve says, to maintain one's hair and ensure its beauty, one must wash it often with her special blend of herbs and leaves."

"Who is Genvieve?" Eyreka asked softly.

"Papa's cousin."

Eyreka could almost feel the unhappiness surround the little one, like the heavy gray smoke of cook's drying fires. As she watched, one crystalline tear slid from the corner of Angelique's eye and flowed in a stream down over her petal-smooth cheek.

"You must miss her."

"She is my only friend," the little girl admitted with a sigh.

"Only?" Eyreka prompted, nearly overcome with emotion that this lonely little girl would show even the tiniest bit of trust by confiding her closely guarded thoughts.

"Aye," Angelique whispered. "With Papa gone so often, the ladies of the court would forget all about me. Without Papa there to return their smiles and place kisses on the backs of their hands as thanks for teaching me to sew or braiding my hair, I became one with the shadows."

Eyreka's heart broke. "But what of Genvieve?"

Angelique brightened. "She never ignored me. She liked me."

Eyreka longed to pull the girl into her arms and soothe away the pain of those past rejections. How many times had Augustin's daughter been rebuffed by the ladies of king William's court?

How many battles had he fought? Her mind answered, dozens ... to both questions.

It was the smallest of sniffles that decided her. Willing to risk rejection by the little girl she so desperately wanted, Eyreka opened her arms.

Angelique hesitated then flung herself into Eyreka's arms. When Eyreka tightened her hold, she burrowed in closer and wept her heart out.

Eyreka's tears mingled with Augustin's daughter's as the two lost souls connected. It was not the same as in her dreams ... dreams in which her own daughter had lived ... but 'twas so very close.

A daughter at last.

Augustin stood rooted to the oaken floor, stricken. His chest ached. He had thought his only daughter safe and well cared for. Instead she had been mistreated and neglected all because of who and what he was.

Bury the past, live the present... Words he now strove to obey. He was wise enough to accept that he could not undo past hurts, but he could change the future. It was in his power to see that his daughter received all of his attention.

He looked at the two women in his life. One, his beloved daughter, the other his wife ... not by choice at first, but now ...

Aye, now ... He let his thoughts drift back to the night before. They had reached a new stage in their relationship, where they were unafraid to admit to the passion between them, and their like need to see the people of Merewood working alongside his warriors...coexisting peacefully. The biggest stumbling block for him had been when she openly admitted her part in the scheme that forced him into marriage. Now, he realized that it no longer mattered. What did matter were her actions since returning to Merewood. She had done all in her power to try to get their two peoples to accept one another. His wife had suffered insults and physical abuse, indirectly because of whom she had married. She was open and honest about her feelings and she truly cared for his men, as if they were her own. Eyreka was honorable, more than deserving of his trust.

The beginnings of that trust would hold their respect for one another in place, while their honor and affection bound them to one another. He was more than pleased with the bargain; Merewood was a wealthy holding, its people respectful. But more than that, he had found something that had been missing from his life for too long. Unable to put the feeling into words, unsure of how to tell her, he merely acknowledged that Eyreka was the force behind the feelings.

Mayhap he should tell her outright what he had come to accept last night, but he was afraid—afraid to give voice to the thought—afraid of her reaction. It was then he felt the power of his wife's gaze upon him. He looked up and was nearly blinded by the beauty of her watery smile. Aye, she was a beauty. His beauty. His, he liked the thought of it.

"She needs me," Eyreka silently mouthed the words.

"I do, too," Augustin mouthed back.

Eyreka watched Augustin silently step back out of the chamber. A heartbeat later, the sound of his footsteps seemed to fill the solar. Angelique pushed away from her, wiping her eyes with the backs of her hands. "Someone comes." Angelique looked toward the door.

"Your father, I believe," Eyreka replied.

"Milady," Augustin said in a rich deep baritone. "Daughter." His smile seemed to soften Angelique's upset at being caught standing too close to her stepmother.

"Is aught amiss?" he asked gently, his gaze taking in the tears clinging to his daughter's long eyelashes.

"'Tis Genvieve," the little one cried. "I have not heard from her in weeks. She was journeying from London with me, when she was called back to tend to her mother."

"I thought only Nadienne, Bernadette, and Simone came with you," Augustin said quietly, holding his daughter close.

"Nay. Genvieve, too," the little one said sadly.

"And you have not heard from her yet?" Eyreka asked, understanding beginning to fill her.

Angelique sighed and shook her head no.

"Mayhap her mother has recovered, but is comforted by Genvieve's presence." Eyreka said wisely.

"I am worried," Angelique confided, looking up at Augustin, and then Eyreka through spiky wet lashes.

"Then I shall send a missive to London asking Genvieve to join us as soon as she is able," Augustin said, in a calm tone.

Sympathy for the girl's plight filled her. Eyreka walked back to her table and straightened her work area, setting aside the dried lavender and mint she was intending to boil for soap. "I am finished for now," she said looking over the top of Angelique's head at Augustin. At his nod of agreement she continued, "Why don't we gather herbs?"

His look of gratitude warmed her.

Angelique shook her head. "I want to ride."

"'Tis too dangerous. Come," she said holding out her hand. "Walk with me."

Angelique grumbled, but followed along. Eyreka knew the child wanted to feel the wind in her hair, the freedom of riding atop a powerful horse. She too longed for it, but until those responsible for trampling their crops had been caught, she would not allow Angelique her freedom.

"Here," she said, kneeling on the cinder path, plucking a sprig of rosemary. "Do you recognize the scent?"

Angelique shrugged, but Eyreka could sense the little one's attitude softening.

"Close your eyes," she urged. "Tell me where you've noticed this scent."

Angelique did as she was bid, closed her eyes and took a deep breath. "Your solar," she answered.

"And?" Eyreka urged.

"The hall …" Angelique's eyes shot open wide. "You sprinkle rosemary on the rushes!"

"Very observant of you."

"Why do you use rosemary?" the child asked.

"I like the way it smells ... 'tis clean."

"My turn," Angelique proclaimed. "Close your eyes."

Eyreka did as she was told, and when prompted, she inhaled deeply, but before she could answer 'twas thyme, Angelique's gasp of shock had her opening her eyes.

She saw two strangers slip through the postern gate. "Who are you?" she demanded.

The men shook their heads at her, motioning for her to be quiet, while the men stealthily crept toward them. Eyreka shot to her feet, pulling Angelique with her. She pushed Angelique behind her and told her to go for help, confident that no one would try to harm either of them within the walls of their home.

She belatedly remembered de Jeaneaux's attack—and his escape. A lump of fear clogged her throat. "Angelique, now!" she ordered through clenched teeth.

Before either of them could move, two more men slipped through the gate. As she opened her mouth to speak, a meaty hand clamped over it, silencing her. She struggled to free herself, but the man's other hand swept around her middle and held her fast. She was well and truly caught.

By Odin! Angelique, she thought wildly. She could not turn around, but heard the girl's whimper of fright.

In a matter of moments, they were outside the safety of the walls...bound and gagged.

Augustin.

Fear's icy fingers traced up Eyreka's spine. She was surrounded by a ragged, dirty looking band of cutthroats who were taking them away from their home.

They were well and truly on their own against twelve men who looked as if slitting Eyreka's throat would give them a great amount of pleasure.

Eyreka reached deep inside for the courage that was flagging faced with the threatening faces that surrounded them. She tried to shift her wrists around and slip one hand free, only to feel the rope tighten and the flesh rub raw.

A movement out of the corner of her eye caught her attention. She stopped struggling and noticed Angelique being roughly flung across a horse. Eyreka tried to scream at the brute who handled her stepdaughter so cruelly but the gag prevented her. White-hot rage swept up through her entire body. She would not let these infidels treat the little girl as if she were no more than a piece of meat brought back from the hunt.

Eyreka tightened every muscle in her body and took off like an arrow loosed from a bow, hitting the unsuspecting brute in the stomach with her head. The man was completely taken by surprise. He doubled over, gasping for breath.

Her head ached, but it was worth the pain, if only to show the men she was no weakling to be handled like a sack of grain. Straightening up, she glared at the man who stalked over toward her. Something in the man's face looked vaguely familiar, but before she could remember where she had seen him, his meaty fist connected with her jaw.

Bright white light flashed in front of her eyes as her stomach lurched and the world went black.

"I CANNOT BELIEVE that you would suggest—"

Whatever Garrick was about to say was interrupted by the warning cry shouted down from the top of the wall.

"'Tis Patrick!" Kelly called down, pointing toward the far side of the lower bailey.

The battered warrior dragged himself toward them, meeting Augustin's gaze. Augustin's blood ran cold with dread, knowing that something disastrous had happened.

"Where are they?" he demanded. "Where is Angelique?"

The big Irishman shook his head slowly, his movements

sluggish. Augustin grabbed him by the elbows and steadied the warrior. "You've come this far," he demanded, "don't black out on me now."

Something flickered in the warrior's eyes, and he seemed to rouse himself enough to speak. "I was on my way over to the herb garden to fetch Lady Eyreka ... Gertie burned her arm ..." he slurred his words together like a drunken man. "The women were bound and gagged ... being carried through the postern gate."

Augustin felt bile rise up his throat. "My daughter?"

Patrick looked at him and almost smiled. "Safe with your wife."

"How could she be safe with only a woman to guard her?" Augustin demanded, before remembering the tale of how Eyreka came to be mistress of Merewood.

"Eyreka is resourceful and strong," Patrick said slowly. "She'll watch out for your little—" He never finished what he was going to say, slumping into a bloody heap at Augustin's feet.

"Georges," he called out, "find Henri!"

Word spread like wildfire; while half of the warriors reinforced the curtain wall, another group was forming a search party for the women.

"Mayhap we will find them before the trail grows cold," Garrick said, watching his wife cuddle their son close to her breast. Augustin watched her finger the bit of amber hanging from a cord about her neck, while tears slipped down her cheeks. She bravely listened to what the men planned in silence.

"Garrick," Augustin said, his voice neutral. "Gather supplies and the second contingent of men."

Garrick nodded and wiped the tears from Jillian's face.

"Georges," Augustin called the silent man to his side. "You will head up our defenses with Kelly and Jacques."

Georges agreed, waiting for the rest of the plan.

"I do not want anyone to go outside these walls until the women are returned unharmed." As he spoke a lone rider approached the curtain wall. Grim determination radiated from the rider. He gave the signal and was allowed entrance. Nodding, he rode straight to Augustin's side. He leaped from his horse and placed a missive in Augustin's hands.

"I cannot stay." The man nervously looked over his shoulder.

"Who is it from?" another of the guard asked.

Augustin broke the wax seal. The words he read hit him like a hammer blow to the chest. His breath snagged, disbelief holding him motionless. They had his wife and daughter!

As Augustin struggled to breathe, the man remounted and slipped past the guard and headed out of the gate. Kelly was off like a shot, but the rider had disappeared. By the time he returned alone, Augustin had read the demand to Garrick and his brother. Aaron the Saxon demanded one hundred pieces of gold for the safe return of the women.

Augustin watched and heartily approved as Garrick's jaw clenched and unclenched while the younger man visibly tried to swallow his anger. "Garrick, you and your men will follow our trail."

Augustin continued, "When you find it, divide your men into two groups. One half should veer off to the east and circle back around, while the other heads west to do the same."

A tall lean warrior stepped forward to speak. "I would go with you, milord," William said quietly.

Augustin looked at the man who a month ago had been ready to accept death as payment for trying to feed his family. The steely determination in the man's eyes, coupled with the rigid control he obviously strove for, decided him.

"Ride with Garrick," he ordered. William nodded and moved off to join the other group of warriors.

Looking at Henri and seeing the worry there had Augustin silently vowing to find the bastards behind the abduction and then skin them alive.

It was not easy to find their trail. There were no signs of a scuffle, no broken tree branches or churned up dirt. About three miles from Merewood, three sets of hoof prints, and at least a dozen sets of footprints, headed to the north. A half mile away, the trail was obliterated by a group of horses' hoof prints. Too many to count.

"They met with reinforcements here." Augustin pointed to where the road had been ground up beneath the heavy animals. They followed the trail to a point where the prints split.

"Which way?" Henri asked.

"I do not know." Augustin clenched his teeth. "We cannot split up, our group is too small."

"Will we wait for Garrick then?" his vassal asked.

Augustin started to shake his head when a bright spot of blue caught his eye. He dismounted, walked over to the hedgerow and pulled off the bit of torn fabric that clung to the short stubby branches. He recognized the color and desperately missed the woman. An image of Eyreka pulling his tunic off sent a shaft of heat through him. Last night in the bathing chamber had been a revelation to him. He held the scrap tightly in his fist for a moment before replacing it on the bush. He would not lose her now that he had realized that he loved her.

"This way," he said motioning the group of warriors.

"What have you got there?" Jean asked.

"My wife was wearing a blue bliaut this morning," he said slowly, "the same blue as her eyes."

Henri snorted and reached past Augustin to grab the fabric. Augustin grabbed his arm saying, "Leave it for Garrick. With luck, he'll find the trail and follow us."

Henri and Jean fell in behind Augustin, who stopped now and again beside the trail they followed to finger another small bit of fabric. As before, Augustin left the bit of blue to mark the way. Patrick was right, he thought, his wife was resourceful, leaving a trail for him to follow.

GARRICK AND HIS men divided at the agreed upon point, circling around and meeting back together after scouting the surrounding area. Though a light rain had started to fall, they were able to follow Augustin's trail, finding each bit of blue fabric as Augustin had hoped they would. By nightfall, his group of men approached a small campsite, and the smell of roasted rabbit hung in the heavy, wet air.

"I'm hungry," Aimory whispered.

Garrick cuffed the younger knight on the back of the head to silence him, and motioned for him to follow along behind. As they silently wound their way closer to the campsite, Garrick had the uneasy feeling that he was being stalked.

The blade at his throat was cold and sharp, the edge of it lying against his Adam's apple.

"Come for dinner?" the familiar voice taunted.

"Augustin!" he rasped.

"Aye," the man answered, "I heard you coming."

"What about the rest of your men?" Garrick asked, feeling the heat of humiliation color his face.

Augustin let him go and shoved him toward the small camp-fire. "They thought I was hearing things."

"I had the feeling someone was behind me," Garrick began.

"I saw the way you tensed up," Augustin said slowly. "Next time, go with your gut instinct and draw your blade."

The younger warrior nodded, taking a seat by the fire, notic-ing it was just hot enough to roast the small bits of meat.

Augustin noticed him looking at the fire. "Any larger and we might attract the wrong attention. I want to surprise them ... not be surprised by them." Augustin tossed him a bit of roasted rabbit and sat down beside him.

Henri stood watch and the others slept. Garrick listened as Augustin went over the plan once more. "If we split up again, we can come at their camp from both sides. With the element of surprise on our side," Augustin said slowly, "they will not know where to defend first. We need a few hours of sleep before we attack."

"At dawn?"

"Nay," Augustin said quietly. "Midnight."

The sounds of Garrick's rhythmic breathing blended in with the rustle of leaves and the erratic call of a night bird. Sleep eluded Augustin. Every time he closed his eyes, he saw a bold Saxon woman, past the first blush of youth, yet all the more beautiful for the wisdom and maturity that added silver to her hair and laugh lines by her eyes.

He rolled onto his back and stared up at the sky. The moon was full, but kept sliding behind the storm clouds that still dotted the sky. He thought of the woman who had pried open the doors to his heart. Though he tried to hold her at arm's length, Eyreka had not been satisfied with the small part of himself that he offered to her. He offered her his body, she held out for his heart. He offered his protection, she was holding out for his love.

As sleep beckoned to him, he relaxed. Drifting off, he thought of how, when he next saw her, he would crush her in his arms and tell her all that was in his heart.

CHAPTER TWENTY-THREE

"WAKE UP!" THE high-pitched voice whispered in her ear. "Before they come back."

Eyreka struggled to rouse herself from a blackness that seemed unnatural. As she opened her eyes, the first thing she saw jarred her back to the present. Angelique's face was inches from her own. A smudge of dirt slashed across the little girl's chin, a purple bruise blossomed beneath her left eye, and her ice-blue eyes were filled with fear.

Eyreka reached up and cupped the side of Angelique's face. "Who hit you, lass?" she asked softly.

"The bad man," she answered, gravely looking over her left shoulder.

Eyreka followed her glance, her gaze resting on the group of men hunched around a small fire, shoveling food into their faces. Any one of them would have fit that description.

"Which one," she asked patiently.

Angelique pursed her mouth and frowned. "The one who hit you."

Totally exasperated, Eyreka raised herself up on one elbow and tried to sound patient, "I did not get a good look at him, can you tell me what he looked like?"

The little girl's eyes widened and then narrowed, as she watched the men. "The one sitting apart from the circle," she whispered, pointing to the largest man in the group.

Eyreka focused on the warrior and felt an icy coldness seep into her bones. Aaron! She recognized him at last. Owen of Sedgeworth's vassal. Fear threatened to overwhelm her, remembering the way Aaron had attacked Garrick's wife ... Jillian had almost died. What could he possibly have to gain by abducting Angelique, she wondered, never even considering that she was the true target.

She sat up and belatedly noticed that she was soaked, "Did it rain?"

Angelique turned back to look at her. Eyreka decided not to tell her that she knew their captor, or that he was a ruthless man who had no conscience ... worse still, he had no soul. She sighed and watched Angelique's midnight black brows arching high before settling into a frown once more. "He hit you hard, didn't he," she asked, sounding concerned.

"Aye." Eyreka rubbed her jaw lightly, but her breath still caught in her throat as a fresh shaft of pain radiated from the left side of her face, all the way up to her temple. "Very hard."

"I've been trying to listen," Angelique confessed, "though I don't know how it will help my idea."

Eyreka almost laughed aloud. Augustin's daughter had backbone ... She had the grit to want to do something about their situation. She decided then and there that she had found a kindred spirit in the little girl. "What idea?" she urged, leaning back against a boulder.

"If we could make the men split up, I could make them chase me." Her bright-blue eyes glowed with excitement. "Then, you hit them on the head with a really, really big stick," Angelique finished solemnly.

Eyreka knew there were many reasons the little girl's plan would not work, but until her addled wits could come up with another plan, she would say nothing. She would cut out her tongue before dashing away the little one's bright smile of hope.

"My other idea did not work though," Angelique said frowning.

"Tell me," Eyreka urged.

"I tore a piece of your bliaut and left bits of it behind to mark our trail."

"Angelique! What a brave thing to do." Eyreka praised her. Then she frowned. "But what if they had caught you?" she asked, silently thanking Odin that their captors had not.

"That's when the bad man hit me," Angelique said softly.

Eyreka wished she could undo the past, but mayhap 'twas all for the best. Angelique would have a blackened eye, but no other injuries, and mayhap help would find them.

"Let us think of a way to distract our captors then." Leaning close to Augustin's daughter, she urged, "And while we are at it, tell me what you've heard."

Angelique repeated almost word for word the conversation she had overheard not one hour past. Their abductors were planning to set a trap for Augustin, and she would be the bait.

Eyreka's heart turned over in her breast. She had to find a way to stop them before Aaron and his band of cutthroats could put their plans into action. She could not bear to think of anything happening to Angelique. Though prickly, the little girl was bright, courageous, and had a wit that rivaled her youngest son's.

"What about Papa?" Angelique asked, after sitting silent for long moments.

The thought of a blade bisecting her husband made her blood run cold. Her stomach lurched in protest as she remembered another brave man who had not been able to escape a like fate. Nay! her mind screamed. I cannot lose him, now that I've found him, she thought. It was then the full force of her feelings rushed through her making her head light and her breath shallow. She was not falling in love with Augustin ... she loved him!

What began as a marriage of necessity, a grand plan to save her family's home, evolved into a union of two lonely people who were learning to love again. Now it looked as if it would end, as it had the first time, with the man she loved being lured into a trap. If she knew Augustin, and she believed she did, he would fight to the last breath ... to the last drop of his warrior's blood.

I cannot let him die, too. There must be a way ... Aaron must have a weakness ... something.

"Eyreka." Angelique shook her arm.

"Aye?"

"'Tis him!" the child whispered, starting to cling to the side of Eyreka's body, before wiggling behind her, until Angelique was wedged between her and the big rock.

"Who?" she demanded.

"Phillipe," the child wailed.

"De Jeaneaux?" Eyreka gasped, a noxious combination of anger and fear washing over her.

She could feel the child vigorously nodding her head.

"You know of him, child?" she asked holding on to her anger, pushing the fear from her mind. Instead, concentrating on the little one who so desperately needed her.

"Aye, he is friend to my papa," she said quietly.

Eyreka felt a shudder rack the little girl's body. She turned around and pulled Angelique into her arms, holding her close to her heart. It felt right. She never thought to have another daughter.

What a fool not to realize that one did not have to bear a child to be a mother to a child. If Angelique was willing, Eyreka thought, she would gladly offer the tiny bit of her heart that belonged to Freya.

Resolving to change that, Eyreka decided to set things aright and vowed to treat Angelique as if she were the daughter of her flesh, not just the daughter of her heart.

Her heart went out to the young girl in her arms. Angelique's mother had died in childbirth; she had never known the love of a mother.

"I have met de Jeaneaux," Eyreka said in a deceptively soft

voice.

"Is it true?" Angelique pulled away from her firm hold and looked up at her.

"Is what true?" she prompted.

"Did he try to ... did he ..." Angelique stopped and hid her face against Eyreka's breast.

The anguish in her voice finished what Angelique could not say. "Who told you?" Eyreka asked, her voice rough with emotion, ready to choke the person who repeated the story to a little girl.

"No one," she answered at last. "I heard Nadienne and Bernadette talking about it."

"Ahh," Eyreka said softly. "What did you hear?"

"That he tried to hurt you with his ... his body," she said in a tiny voice.

"Aye," Eyreka said knowing that the two Norman maidservants would have used more coarse words to describe the near-rape, but it was close enough.

"Why would a friend of Papa's try to hurt you?" The look in Angelique's eyes showed her confusion.

"Not all men are as honorable as your father," she began. "Augustin de Chauret is honest and loyal," Eyreka realized now was the time for truth. "Though he did not want to wed again, I made a bargain with the king, and your papa honored it."

"Why did he marry you?"

"When I found out that my family's home was being deeded over to a widowed Norman baron, I offered myself as wife." Eyreka wanted to offer an uncomplicated explanation, one that would be easy for Angelique to understand.

"Why didn't he refuse?" the little one persisted.

"Because I convinced the king that Merewood Keep's people would accept your father as lord if I were to be his wife. Not even your father would dare to refuse the king."

Angelique nodded her understanding. Though but ten summers, the child was smart as a whip. "But you love him," she whispered.

"Aye, little one," Eyreka said, tears flowing down her cheeks. "With all my heart."

"Then I will learn to love you, too," Angelique shocked Eyreka by hugging her tight.

AUGUSTIN GAVE THE signal. The group divided and moved silently toward the fire that blazed against the black of night. The rain stopped. The clouds opened, allowing the full moon to lend an added glow of light, enabling the men to see their prey. Garrick led the group heading off to the left of the encampment, while Augustin led the rest of the men around to the other side. Once his men were in place, Augustin tilted his head to listen for the screech of an owl ... Garrick's signal.

When he heard it, Augustin threw back his head and screamed his own battle cry. The night came alive, humming with sound, as the echoing bone-chilling cry was heard. Garrick, he thought proudly. Augustin and his men charged.

Chaos erupted in front of them as men scrambled to their feet, reaching for their weapons. Augustin raced toward them, his sword arm already descending in a deadly arch.

"Papa!"

His daughter's scream cut through the familiar sounds of battle, making the hair on his scalp prickle. He spun about on the balls of his feet, ready for the attacker that leaped toward him with arms raised high above his head two-handing his broadsword. Augustin brought his own sword up from beneath his attacker. The man was dead before he hit the ground. But before he could extract his sword, another warrior moved in for the kill. His death would be swift, Augustin thought.

He pulled his sword free and moved to deflect the killing blow. It never came. William had run his sword through the infidel. Before Augustin could nod his thanks, he heard Eyreka cry out, "Archer ... to your left!"

He threw himself to the ground, and used the momentum to roll to the edge of the campsite. An arrow quivered, stuck in the tree behind where he had stood moments before. Had he not heeded Eyreka's warning cry, he would be skewered to that tree ... dead.

Looking over his shoulder at his men engaged in battle, he saw that the odds were dwindling on the side of the infidels and rapidly gaining in their favor. As his gaze swept the forest around him, he saw a light-haired man grab Eyreka. He'd thought her safe. Then watched her valiant effort to fight him off, despite the fact that her attacker was nearly thrice her size. He silently cheered her on when she kneed the man ... but her attacker did not fall to his knees, he let out a roar of anger.

"Nay!" Angelique cried out, leaping toward the Saxon who attacked Eyreka. As Augustin ran toward them, he saw his daughter kicking and clawing for all she was worth. *Mon Dieu*, he thought, do not let him hurt her. As he raced to the other side of the clearing, a familiar voice called out, stopping him cold.

"So you did come after your wife," de Jeaneaux sounded surprised. "I was wrong."

"And my daughter," Augustin added seeing Garrick out of the corner of his eye. He nodded and Garrick started to move in from the other side. Augustin was relieved that Eyreka's son had been gifted with his mother's quick mind.

"Your daughter?" Phillipe ground out. "The one you spoke of so often?"

"Aye," Augustin said, circling the warrior. "Who did you think the child was?"

"Your Saxon wife's," de Jeaneaux bit out.

"Nay, look closely, you will see that she is a miniature of her mother, Monique," Augustin said quietly. She has reflexes like her stepmother though, he thought watching the little one try to land one more swift kick to de Jeaneaux's shins.

"You said the child belonged to the Saxon!" de Jeaneaux shouted at Aaron, who stood straddling Eyreka. That split second was all Augustin needed, he sprang forward, intending to carve a piece out of the Norman infidel. But at the last second, de Jeaneaux swung back around and deflected the force of the blow.

Before Augustin could make a grab for his daughter, the huge warrior, who had so brutally handled his wife, stepped forward out of the shadows and lunged for his daughter. When Angelique eluded him, the warrior moved forward to strike out at her.

"Aaron!" de Jeaneaux bellowed. "Not the child!"

She danced out of his reach again. Incensed, Aaron drew his broadsword and leaped toward the little girl.

De Jeaneaux pushed the child behind him, catching Aaron's blade in his thigh. He crumbled under the force of the blow.

"Augustin!" Garrick shouted, "On your right!"

Augustin dove to the left, landing on his weak hip. He felt the muscles start to give, but he ground his teeth together and ignored the pain. Rising to his knees, he was ready to fend off the last of the attackers. As his blade connected and the man slid to the ground, he heard Angelique scream. The unholy sound made his heart wrench in his breast. He turned toward the sound of her voice and froze in absolute horror.

The madman who had dared to abduct his women had his broadsword raised above his head, ready to slice down into his little girl. Bile rushed up his throat at the realization that he was too far away to save her.

"No!" Eyreka screamed, flinging a rock at Aaron's raised arm, forcing it to the side, before throwing herself in front of Angelique.

Chapter Twenty-Four

Never before had the carnage of battle affected Augustin, but the sickening sound of Aaron's blade parting Eyreka's milk-white flesh would stay with him forever.

For one horrible moment, time stood still, as his wife gracefully fainted dead away at the madman's feet. Augustin's roar of anguish echoed through the camp as he drove his broadsword through Aaron's unprotected side.

"Papa," Angelique wailed. "Do something!"

Augustin gathered his wife in his arms and carried her over to the fire. Laying her out on the ground, he tore a strip from her chainse and started to bind her wound.

A small grubby hand stopped him. "We must clean it out first," Angelique said quietly.

"She'll lose too much blood," he said gently moving his daughter out of the way. While he held the cloth against the bloody gash in her side, Garrick knelt down next to him.

"Angelique is right," Garrick said in a firm voice. "I may not have had the time to learn all that my mother knows about healing," he said quietly, "but I do know the wound must be clean, or she'll catch wound-fever."

Augustin barely heard what Garrick said to him, his focus was on the woman he loved. *Merde.* He never had the chance to tell her how he felt. *Don't take her from me, too.* Too engrossed in

BARGAINING WITH THE LADY OF MEREWOOD

his thoughts to notice what was going on around him, he was surprised when a clean little hand stilled his ministrations.

"Papa," Angelique said. "Let me. I know what to do."

While he watched, his daughter ripped pieces of her own bliaut off, discarding the bottom edge. She dipped the clean strips in the bucket of water that had been heating for their captor's supper. Angelique worked awkwardly, but swiftly.

Once she had the wound cleansed to Garrick's satisfaction, he nodded and finally spoke, "It will need to be sewn."

"We have to get back to the holding," Augustin said quietly. "We'll need Eyreka's needle, threads, and healing herbs." He took his daughter's hands in his. Hers were so tiny, almost birdlike, and so very cold. His were massive in comparison and rough from years of wielding a broadsword.

"The wound must be tightly bound," he instructed. He helped Angelique fold the strips of linen into a thick pad and placed it directly on the gash. Then they wound more strips all the way around Eyreka's middle.

Garrick's gaze met his and understanding flowed between them. They had worked closely together to find the women, and now they worked together to save Eyreka's life.

Augustin remembered the gentle touch his daughter used on his wife. There was no doubt the child had been changed by what she had seen. Gone was the petulant, spoiled little girl. In her place was a caring young woman who had the gift of healing. He had a feeling that Angelique would watch over her new mother very carefully. His daughter had much to learn from his wife. After all, Eyreka had taught him to love again, mayhap she could teach his daughter what it meant to have a mother's love.

He would never forget the way Eyreka had saved his daughter's life, or the image of Eyreka throwing her body in front of the blade meant for his little girl.

"Augustin?" Henri's voice broke through his troubled thoughts.

"Aye?"

"What should I do with the bodies?"

Looking around him, he noticed a dozen bodies strewn about the campsite. The trees were lush, and the scent of pine heavy in the air. The thought of leaving the bodies to defile the beauty of the forest did not seem right. Though the infidels did not deserve it, he gave the order, "Bury them."

Henri nodded his head and started to turn away. "She will need her comfrey poultice," he said gruffly.

His vassal's words touched him deeply. Henri had not loudly proclaimed to accept the Saxon woman Augustin had married, but it was there in his concern for her injury.

"Mayhap you could carry my daughter—" Augustin began.

Garrick interrupted him, "Nay, Henri's arm is still weak, I'll carry Angelique."

When Augustin nodded, Garrick continued, "You can carry my mother."

The trust was there in the younger warrior's voice. Garrick was entrusting his mother to Augustin, and the meaning had not been lost on him. He had been accepted at last. "She will recover," Augustin said firmly, leaving no room for argument.

As the weary party of warriors carried their precious burdens, the sun broke over the horizon. The dawn of a new day greeted them as they headed home toward Merewood Keep.

Eyreka stirred, feeling as if she were floating adrift on a soft white cloud. Everything she looked at seemed to be just slightly out of focus, unreal.

Augustin held her in his arms, his grip strong and sure. He had come to rescue them, she thought. Through her lowered lashes, she recognized Merewood's familiar curtain wall, as they rode through the gate. She sighed. Her love was bringing her home, she thought as the soft white air darkened, and she slipped into the blessed darkness where there was no pain.

"Papa," Angelique called out sleepily. "Promise she'll be all right."

"I promise." He prayed fervently that God would not leave

him without the woman he loved a second time.

WHITE-HOT PAIN SEARED through Eyreka's side, waking her. She moaned and tried to move, but was held still by strong hands. As she struggled the rest of the way to consciousness, she remembered the blade headed for Angelique's heart.

"Angelique!" she cried out, trying to break free of the hands that held her.

"Be still!" The deep timbre of her husband's voice flowed over her, soothing her like honeyed wine.

Another sharp pain jabbed into her side. She bit down on her bottom lip, unwilling to make a sound.

"Could you not have had the good sense to remain unconscious while Kelly sewed you back together, wife?" Augustin bit out.

"I wish I had," she whimpered. So many times she had been the one to mend jagged edges of flesh, caring for Merewood's people. It was the first time she herself had to suffer through it.

"Mayhap a goblet of mead would ease the pain." She gasped, as the needle poked through her skin again.

"Angelique," he called.

His daughter carried over a goblet and while Augustin propped Eyreka up, Angelique held the cup to her lips.

The thick sweet mead soothed her parched throat. Pulling away from the cup, she forced herself to smile. "My thanks."

"Does it hurt a lot?" Angelique asked, her eyes round with trepidation.

Eyreka closed her eyes against the pain and nodded. "A lot."

"As much as the blade?" Angelique whispered.

Eyreka opened her eyes and looked at the little girl. "I would do anything to protect the ones I love," she said with conviction.

Tears flowed freely down the child's pale white cheeks. Angelique used her sleeve to wipe at her watery eyes and runny nose. "How can you love me?" she asked. "I've been so mean to you."

As Kelly tied the last knot and began to bandage her side, Eyreka held out her hand to the little girl.

"Sometimes when you are lonely, or you lose someone close to you, a terrible anger fills your heart. You cannot help striking out at others while the pain and hurt fester inside of you."

"Fester?" Angelique asked.

"Aye, when a wound goes bad," Eyreka explained.

Angelique scrunched her nose and said, "I've seen that happen." Then she added, "It is horrible to look at!"

Eyreka nodded. "But with care and patience, you can cleanse the wound, and it will heal." She looked up and caught Augustin staring at her, the look in his eyes made her want to weep with joy. Her husband understood that she not only spoke of wounds of the flesh, but wounds of the heart as well.

Angelique climbed up onto the bed and snuggled next to Eyreka's uninjured side. The poor little thing took one deep breath and sniffled loudly.

As Eyreka smoothed the shiny black hair off Angelique's forehead, and heard the child's breathing slow down, becoming deeper and even.

"She sleeps," Augustin said.

"She has been through an ordeal." Eyreka defended her. "She is so young."

"As young as you," Augustin said, "when you bravely stood before your father's captors."

Eyreka felt the warmth of his words flow through her.

"She may have night terrors," Eyreka warned.

"Did you?" he asked pointedly.

She nodded her head slowly. "For the first year of my marriage to Addison."

"And who soothed your fears away?" Augustin asked, his stomach knotting with the unfamiliar feeling of jealousy.

"My husband," she answered. "He was a powerful warrior, an arrogant man."

Augustin snorted loudly.

"But he was honest, and I knew I could trust him." Eyreka stared at the scar on Augustin's face and remembered the wicked one that sliced across his chest. Her husband carried many marks of valor on the outside; she wondered how many he carried on the inside. Mayhap she could help him to heal.

"'Twas one of the first things I noticed about you, Augustin," she said softly. "You are an arrogant man, and a strong warrior."

"But?" he prompted, raising his gaze to meet hers. His eyes hardened with anger.

"You treated our people fairly from the start," she continued. "You never blindly sided with your men. You always listened to both sides before passing judgment. My people have come to trust you," she whispered, "as I have come to trust you."

She blinked away the tears that blurred her husband's image. "You are a man of passion and honor." She looked away from his intense stare and let her gaze rest upon his daughter. "I have come to care deeply for your daughter," she said, looking back at him, "but I have grown to love her father."

"You do?" he whispered brokenly.

"With all my heart," she rasped.

He pulled her carefully into his arms and pressed his lips to hers. His love poured through the kiss, filling in the empty spaces of her heart, until Eyreka was filled to bursting with wonder.

She felt tears running down her face, but ignored them, cupping the side of his face with her hand. "I never thought to find love a second time, Augustin," she said softly. "I loved Addison with a young girl's hopes and ideals." At his dark look she stroked his brow, easing the tension in his face. "But I love you with a woman's heart and the wisdom that comes from surviving the journey of life."

"Eyreka," Augustin whispered, placing a gentle kiss on her forehead, one on the tip of her nose and finally her mouth. "I closed myself off from love when Monique died in my arms after struggling to deliver our babe." His voice broke, but he cleared his throat and continued. "Monique was beautiful with a gentle heart. She was fragile. My need to protect her, and see her safe, was almost as strong as my love for her.

"After she died, I would not allow another woman close enough to touch my heart." He stroked the tips of his fingers across her cheek and along the line of her jaw. "I could not bear to love again, knowing that the one I loved could be cruelly ripped from me. I tried to not to love you, but I could not hold out against your strength, your courage, and your gift for embracing life."

His stormy-gray eyes were filled with hope as they searched her ice-blue eyes for the answer. Their gazes met and held, stormy gray softening to a warm deep gray; ice blue changing to a soft clear blue.

He saw beyond his prejudices and those of their two warring peoples to a peaceful coexistence. "You are my life," he rasped.

This time when she looked into his eyes she didn't see the specter of a departed love; she saw a second chance at happiness. She pressed her lips to his and whispered, "And you are my love."

Augustin bowed his head and gave thanks for the gifts in his life, Angelique and Eyreka, and held them close to his heart. Pressing his lips to Eyreka's temple he rasped, "I'd like to tell you about my home."

Epilogue

A few weeks later...

WITH EACH DAY that passed, peace settled over Merewood Keep. Augustin marveled that he had grown to love his wife more with each passing day.

His life and that of his daughter were richer, their love deeper and fuller all because of the courage, forgiveness, and love of the woman who held his heart. He watched Eyreka from the open doorway to his daughter's bedchamber and was awed at how quickly his world seemed to right itself. He no longer held tightly to the past, or blamed himself for his first wife's death, nor for not knowing his daughter was being treated shabbily when he was not at court.

The Lady of Merewood had helped him believe again. Had taught him that her love was unconditional. No matter if they had differing opinions, disagreed, or shared harsh words between them, she taught him a simple, heartfelt apology oftentimes was all that was needed. He had gained much more than a home to raise his daughter when the king gifted him the holding of Merewood Keep—he'd gained a wife and strong sons. Sons who followed their mother's example and laid aside their hatred of all things Norman, accepting him as their overlord and stepfather. He'd been infinitely blessed. Fierce love for his new family twined with the love he had for his daughter. He was stronger because of it.

He must have made a sound from where he stood in the doorway. Angelique turned toward him and smiled. "I'm ready for you to kiss me goodnight, Papa!"

Augustin walked toward her bed. Smiling, he bent down and pressed a kiss to her forehead and the tip of her nose. Angelique's eyes were already closing when he whispered, "Sleep well, *ma petite ange*." Her breathing slowed as she fell into a deep sleep.

"Come." He tugged on his wife's hand, urging her to follow him out of the bedchamber. But her mere touch was not enough. He pulled Eyreka into his arms, and still the feel of her curves fitted against the hard planes of his warrior's body was not enough. He needed to feel her warmth and the beat of her heart—skin to skin. He dipped his head and pressed a kiss to her lips, trailing more along the line of her jaw to just beneath her ear. "Are you ready for me to kiss you goodnight, my love?"

She tilted her head back and met his stormy-gray gaze. "I'm not sleepy."

God, how he needed to make love to her! He groaned, scooped her into his arms, and strode to their bedchamber. Shoving the door open with his shoulder, he stepped inside with his precious burden and kicked the door closed behind him.

"Give me time, and you will be."

His lips met hers in a soul-searing kiss that promised of forever.

About the Author

In case we have not met yet, here is a little bit about me:
I write Historical & Contemporary Romance featuring: Hard-headed Heroes & Feisty Heroines.

I fell in love at first sight at seventeen, with the man who will hold my heart forever. DJ and I were married for forty-one wonderful years until my darling lost his battle with cancer. We have three grown children—one son-in-law, two grandsons, two rescue dogs, two rescue grand-cats, and one rescue grand-puppy.

My Hardheaded Heroes and Feisty Heroines rarely listen to me. In fact, I think they enjoy messing with my plans for them. BUT if there is one thing I've learned in dealing with my characters for the past twenty-nine years, it is to listen to them! My heroes always have a few of DJ's best qualities: his honesty, his integrity, his compassion for those in need, and his killer broad shoulders.

I have always used family names in my books and love adding bits and pieces of my ancestors and ancestry in them, too. I write about the things I love most: my family, my Irish and English ancestry, baking and gardening.

Happy reading!

Sláinte!
CH

C.H.'s Social Media Links:

Website: www.chadmirand.com
Amazon: amazon.com/stores/C.-H.-Admirand/author/B001JPBUMC
BookBub: bookbub.com/authors/c-h-admirand
Facebook Author Page: facebook.com/CHAdmirandAuthor
GoodReads:
goodreads.com/author/show/212657.C_H_Admirand
Dragonblade Publishing: dragonbladepublishing.com/team/c-h-admirand
Instagram: instagram.com/c.h.admirand
Twitter: @AdmirandH
Youtube:
youtube.com/channel/UCRSXBeqEY52VV3mHdtg5fXw

Milton Keynes UK
Ingram Content Group UK Ltd.
UKHW021009061024
449204UK00010B/517